Hard to Get By

(Book Four of the Hard to Get Series)

by Jenny Gardiner

http://jennygardiner.net/

What people are saying about Jenny Gardiner's books:

Red Hot Romeo
"Awesome". So enjoyed the romantic chemistry between the two characters. Read it non stop into the wee hours. Highly recommend this book
-- Mrs. K

Blue-Blooded Romeo
"Another brilliant, fun read from Jenny Gardiner. The book is fun to read and I thoroughly enjoyed every word. Jenny Gardiner has put the fun back into romance books and I look forward to each book in this delightful series."
-- Anne Blyth

"I had planned on only reading a few chapters at first but couldn't put it down. A terrific storyline, well-developed and extremely relatable characters, what's not to love?? Great read!"
-- Samantha Reeves

Big O Romeo
"I could not put this book down. Warning don't start this book late at night as you will not want to stop reading.
-- Di

Sleeping with Ward Cleaver
"A fun, sassy read! A cross between Erma Bombeck and Candace Bushnell, reading Jenny Gardiner is like sinking your teeth into a chocolate cupcake...you just want more."
--Meg Cabot, NY Times bestselling author of Princess

Diaries, Queen of Babble and more

Slim to None
"Jenny Gardiner has done it again--this fun, fast-paced book is a great summer read."
--Sarah Pekkanen, NY Times bestselling author of *The Opposite of Me*

Chapter One

Two Years Earlier

MEGHAN Ferguson had had it with work. As cool as her job sounded on paper, in reality, being a press secretary to a U.S. senator was all-consuming, and when it came time for re-election, it went from bad to worse. Only the dirty truth was, it was always re-election season. There wasn't a politician to be found in the Washington, D.C. area who wasn't campaigning for a job or appointment or another cushy six years with great government benefits and freebies out the wazoo twenty-four/seven. All they did was jockey for more, more, more. The DC gravy train kept them fat and happy. And it was lowly staffers like Meghan who suffered for it. Cause it meant that Meghan spent her waking hours churning out steaming heaps of bullshit trying to make her high-maintenance boss look good. And when they were legit in the battle for re-election, it was that much worse, because then she constantly had to deal with the bombardment of slurs hurled at her boss from his opponent — make that more often his opponent's press secretary — and it all just got quite exhausting. It used to be sort of exhilarating, but now it was just hellish, and a bit depressing.

She'd been working in publicity for the senator for the better part of the last decade, and she was spent. Today had been a long day. Her boss' challenger had held a press event earlier, in advance of a debate tomorrow night, at which he referred to the senator as a "dimwitted womanizing loser" or some such drivel. The senator flipped his shit over that one (and while he wasn't necessarily dimwitted, or a loser, he was certainly a creeper of a womanizer). Worse still, the challenger's publicist even called out Meghan as an inept press secretary who spread lies and misinformation. Even she was seething by the time she'd turned off the presser, and was this close to marching to wherever it was their headquarters were and telling his newest press person (the candidate seemed to have trouble keeping one in his employ for long) to cut the crap. Because that person could control this behavior and was failing to do so.

Which was possibly why she found herself having one too many cocktails on her own at Bottoms Up, her favorite little local near her Capitol Hill rowhouse, and becoming engrossed in conversation with a handsome stranger who held tightly to every word she uttered. It was kind of nice for a guy to give her his undivided attention, even if whatever she was blathering on about was complete nonsense.

At the moment her witty repartee had to do with the desperate need for another baby panda at the National Zoo, because, well, it was a conversation about as far away from politics as possible, which was exactly what she needed. And a baby panda would be something she could obsess on rather than how much of a loathsome bully her boss was. Earlier in the day, before that debacle of a presser, the senator had reamed her for something he'd said that he decided to blame her for — because isn't that how it worked? Accountability was apparently for underlings. She was just over the whole damned thing.

She'd taken on this job with absolutely no political skills whatsoever. She'd been working for a local television station in a miniature media market and yearned to be in a city. So, she ditched her reporting aspirations and took a job for which she had no great qualifications, except for bullshitting quite successfully during her job interview.

"Maybe instead of breeding pandas, the National Zoo should breed something more exotic, like blue whales," the cute guy next to her said with a grin. He had gorgeous, straight, white teeth. That worked well with his thick, light brown hair and eyes that vacillated between green and golden. Or maybe that was her third mojito that was seeing that. Cause who had golden eyes but for lions. Or billy goats?

She swatted the cute guy on the shoulder. "That's impossible," she said. "Blue whales are, like, ginormous. They weigh over three hundred thousand pounds! What're they going to do — have a holding pen in the Potomac River? And where do you get the mate for the girl blue whale?" She leaned closer to his ear. "Not gonna lie: I'd pay good money to watch two blue whales go at it — it seems like an impossible task! Once we were at a bar in Ocean City and stood on the back deck overlooking the bay and watched thousands of Horseshoe crabs mate. It might have been the alcohol that made it fascinating, but whatever, it kept me mesmerized. That sword thingy, gets in the way." She jutted her arm out from her nose, imitating it.

Meghan started to laugh and tapped the bar so the bartender would fill her up ASAP. She tucked a few strands of blonde hair that had escaped from her tight bun behind her ears, then thought better of it and pulled the hair pins and elastic band out, freeing her long hair and giving her head a vigorous shake. She hadn't realized it was bringing on a headache until now.

The guy pulled out his phone. "We have to see how they do this."

Meghan saw him typing into his browser, "Blue Whale Sex."

She rolled her eyes. "Are we seriously going to watch blue whales fornicate now?"

"Hell, yeah!" He laughed, then began to read. "...they begin to form pairs, where a male will follow a female around for weeks on end...though sex is not a foregone conclusion."

Meghan wagged her finger. "Dude, let me tell you: my girl ain't putting out for just any old blue whale. Even if he does stalk her. She's gonna hold out for a well-endowed whale—"

"...sometimes a second male will approach the pair, at which point the trio will race along the surface of the water."

"I'm sorry, but you best not be suggesting a blue whale threesome. That would displace like half the water in the ocean." She took a swig of her drink. "Besides, this chick is not a promiscuous whale."

"Yeah, well, just like everything else in nature, the guys fight, and whoever wins gets the girl."

"What female wants to end up with the pugnacious asshole, though, as if he's the prize?" She shook her head. "I mean really. What a stupid system." She rolled her eyes.

"Maybe it's more romantic than that," he said. "Maybe it's that these two strapping, male, uh, leviathans, want her so much they're willing to fight to the death for her. Or maybe one is defending her honor when the other one insults her."

"You mean like he called her fat?" She parroted her hands like a puppet talking. "'Hey tubby, you better lay off the krill, sweetheart.'" She growled and rolled her eyes. "Men are the same the world over."

Meghan had recently gotten out of a relationship with a guy she'd dated since college. He actually had told her one time she needed to lose a few pounds or he'd leave her. She should have left him then and there, but she dragged it out longer until she found out he had been two-timing her with a girl three years younger than her from her sorority who'd recently moved to DC. How was that for sisterhood? Whatever. She didn't need that kind of toxic juju in her life. Maybe she needed to find herself a well-endowed blue whale instead.

The guy frowned. "I resemble that comment," he said. "Not all men are assholes."

She nodded, plucking a maraschino cherry from the nearby fruit station at the bar, and popping it into her mouth. "Okay fine. Not all of them. Only ninety-nine point nine, nine, nine percent of them."

She chewed on the cherry and swallowed it, then stuck the stem in her mouth, twisting it with her tongue and her teeth till she secured it in a knot, then pulled it out of her mouth. It looked like a tiny pretzel.

"Ta da!"

The cute guy's eyes opened wide. "Whoa! You did that? With your tongue?"

She laughed to herself. She certainly didn't use someone else's tongue! Though likely his own tongue would be hanging out, drooling at the notion of someone with such lingual dexterity.

She waved her hand. "An old party trick. Used to keep the free drinks flowing at parties."

"Aren't drinks always free at parties?"

She shrugged. "Good point. Maybe that skill didn't help me as much as I thought it did." She grabbed another cherry and repeated the stunt. "Nevertheless, I figured it was a talent I could employ when desperation set in."

"And you're feeling desperate?"

She shook her head. "Nah, just, oh, I dunno, in the mood to tie a cherry stem with my tongue."

"Can you teach me how to do that?"

"Hmmm…" She pursed her lips. "You have to pinky swear if you succeed that you'll not share this with anyone. Only a select few can join the club."

He arched a brow. "Ahhh… it's like a secret society?"

She nodded, pulled another cherry as the bartender scowled at her, and stuck the cherry in her mouth.

She gave a hard tug on the uncomfortable underwire of her bra, sat up straighter, then held up her pointer finger. "Okay, first off, you need to have a long stem."

"The bigger the better, then?"

Her mouth lifted at one end. "That goes without saying."

"Are we talking about the same thing here?"

"If you have to ask…"

He windshield-wipered his hands as if erasing the discussion. "Continue."

"Obviously you have to pop the cherry gingerly." She burst out laughing.

"I had no idea this was going to be such a sexual thing."

"Everything is sexual. Even blue whales." She knit her brows. "Well, maybe not baby pandas."

He shrugged.

"Now this is counterintuitive, but if it's stiff, you want to make it soft."

"Well, that is totally *not* sexual."

"Truth." She high-fived him. "Rarely is limp good. Okay, now's when your tongue gets busy." She could see his eyes growing wide. She was having fun fucking around with his head. She also kind of worried she'd grown too hardened and cynical with her job that she would talk this way to a complete stranger in a bar because she was so fried from work. But oh well…she was too fried to even contemplate that notion.

"Press the center of the stem to the roof of your mouth with your tongue, forcing the two ends toward your front teeth. You're going to clamp down on them as you sort of force them to criss-cross with your tongue, forming a little loop. Then you take one tip and coax it through the hole—"

"This is definitely no longer PG-rated conversation."

"We're talking about cocktail fruit."

"But are we, though?"

She squinted at him. "Honey, I don't even know you." She laughed. "Now push the stiff part of the stem into the hole, then press down with your teeth to secure it. *Et voila*," she swept her hand with a demonstrative flourish, "you have a tied stem that will make all of your friends green, not cherry red, with envy." She quickly popped the straight stem into her mouth, tied it in a matter of seconds, and held it aloft for him to see.

The cute guy leaned forward, his lips inches from her ear. "In about three seconds flat I'm afraid my tongue is going to be green with envy that that inanimate cherry stem is having all the fun around here."

Ahhh… the moment of truth. Until now, Meghan was entertained just by yanking this guy around. But he was awfully cute. And had a fun sense of humor. And when he got up close to her like that, he smelled rather delicious — like a crazy good combination of sandalwood and the Mediterranean Sea and maybe a hint of bergamot and lime. Although that lime was likely just her mojito. Whatever.

Hard to Get By

Maybe it would be fun just to see what he tasted like too. She grabbed one more cherry, stuffing it into his mouth. "Meet me at the end of that hall, just after the exit to go downstairs to the rest rooms." She tapped the tip of his nose with her tied cherry stem and hopped off the barstool.

Chapter Two

HOLY shit. Was she for real? Well, yes, she was for real in that she was unbelievably beautiful — that wavy, blonde hair, once she pulled it out of that tight bun, made Kirby McCaffrey want to fist his hands in it while doing unspeakable things with her. And those aquamarine eyes, so clear you could see down to her soul. Her body was nothing to scoff at either — granted she was sitting so he couldn't quite tell the whole effect, but she had a nice set of tits. And Kirby was decidedly a breast man, so that's all he needed to stir things up. But when she got up and walked away and he was able to take in the bigger picture, *yowza*. She was stunning, with that form-fitting wrap dress hugging her ass, and those sexy heels that weren't too high, but instead looked professional, which is the look he preferred. Not stripper heels, which left nothing to the imagination.

He couldn't believe the turn of fortune he was experiencing tonight. Never in history had such a cartoonishly unnatural piece of pseudo-fruit become such a turn-on. He almost felt like a pervert, like he just discovered he had a cocktail fruit fetish or something. He'd recently heard some quasi-cute "star" of a reality TV program boasting in a podcast that she makes good money selling pictures and videos of her bare feet smashed in Jell-O and he'd made a mental note to never be that kind of weirdo that would pay strange women to do even stranger things to advance his sexual agenda. And maraschino cherries turning you on would totally check that weirdo box. Ugh. But clearly it wasn't the cherry but rather the tongue that was making his pants a bit tighter by the minute.

He looked at the bartender, who tossed him another cherry. "Go get 'em, boss." The guy said with a grin. Was it that obvious? He had to wait a minute at least to tamp down the burgeoning hard-on that was making it hard to stand. But he couldn't risk her sneaking out a fire exit, so he stood, took a deep breath and advanced the troops, as it were.

He wandered down the narrow, dark hallway, passing a few folks returning from the bathroom. He walked past the door to the kitchen and then the passageway grew dimmer still. His eyes adjusted to the dark and he looked about ten feet away and she was standing there, waiting for him.

He approached her and removed the stem from the cherry, slipping the fruit between her lips as he took in the stem between his, manipulating it with the tip of his tongue with no success.

"Let me help," she said, leaning forward and slipping her tongue inside his mouth, coaxing the stem away with her tongue. Somehow as she stroked his tongue with her own, she managed to maneuver the stem into a knot, then passed it back to his mouth. "See. I told you my party trick could come in handy." She grinned.

He pulled her closer and angled his head as he pressed his lips to hers, savoring the tiny moan she let out as their tongues tangled, taking the place of that now-discarded cherry stem. Kirby ran his hands up and down the woman's back, trying to find purchase somewhere, anywhere. His mind was running crazy with longing and while he couldn't believe he was suddenly mashing faces with this strange, gorgeous woman in the grimy back of a bar, he wished he was doing it within footsteps of her bedroom. Or his. Any port in a storm.

She paused for a moment, breathing hard. "I don't even know your name," she said, her eyes looking momentarily startled. "Although maybe it's better that way."

Was she suggesting anonymous sex? Which sounded alluring, but he wanted to know more about this woman, not just have a wham-bam moment with her.

"I make it a point not to get past first base without knowing a woman's name," he said, reaching for her bottom and pulling her toward the telltale bulge in his pants.

"So, is that what this is — first base? Making out wildly in a dive bar in the dark?"

"Maybe the bases are loaded, and we're waiting for that swing and a hit to send that fly ball into the stands?"

She shook her head. "Sorry, no home run tonight. Not simply because I still don't know your name — although that's the primary reason, but also because my boss has a big debate tomorrow. I've got to get some shut-eye cause tomorrow's going to be a long day." She pulled back and extended her hand to shake his. "Name's Meghan, by the way."

He squinted. Fuck to the fuck. She was seriously about to walk away, leaving him with a bad case of blue balls for his troubles? Impossible.

"Meghan. I'm Kirby. Can I maybe get your number and we can get together some time?" Fact was he, too, had a crazy day tomorrow, as his new boss also had a debate. Only in a town like DC would you have a coincidence like that.

She waved her hand. "Thanks, but I'm really not interested in anything. I just got a little carried away. Must've been the maraschino cherries. Or the copulating blue whales. Whatever. Great meeting you, Kirby. Have a good life."

Hard to Get By

With that she turned and walked away, leaving Kirby to groan and curse his bad luck. Then again, this was his first week in Washington, and his boss scored big points at his presser today, and he got to make out with a hot woman for no apparent reason. No reason not to see this as a win.

Chapter Three

MEGHAN kept thinking about that Kirby guy the whole day long. Even as she nursed a mojito-induced hangover, still he was lurking in the recesses of her throbbing head. Speaking of throbbing, it was impossible not to notice the guy was packing an impressive appendage. Maybe she should've taken that thing out for a test run. Except that she didn't have time for boys and their toys right now. Work was all-consuming, and she and men didn't mix well. A fleeting handful of kisses in the dark with a stranger would have to do.

Her desk phone buzzed and she picked it up.

"The senator wants you down here now!" It was Theresa, the senator's bitchy and demanding secretary, happy to yell into the phone and accelerate her pounding headache. God forbid she start out the call with something a bit more genteel. Like maybe "Hey, Meghan! How's it going? I'm sorry to bother you but just FYI the senator is being a raging asshole right now, and he's screaming for you, like, yesterday. Good luck and I'll keep you in my prayers!"

Instead, she just served as his surrogate of vitriol, cobbling yet one more roadway of nastiness that Meghan had to navigate her way through, trying not to break a metaphorical ankle along the way.

She grabbed her iPad, her purse and her notes and raced down the steps and into the senator's private suite.

Hard to Get By

"Where the hell were you? I was yelling for you! Don't you come when you're called?" The Senator had a scowl on his face, as usual. A long strand of his bad combover was dangling, noodle-like, on his forehead, and he looked like Squiggy from that old show *Laverne & Shirley*, with the bad shoe polish-black hair color. She never understood why people didn't notice how preposterous and unnatural a harsh black dye looked on the head of an obviously older person. Ditto the spaghetti hair hiding the bald pate.

She straightened her dress and combed her fingers through her hair. "Sorry, sir. I came as quickly as I could."

"Where are my talking points?" he stepped into his bathroom, not even shutting the door, and started to pee. What was proper protocol for when your boss didn't have the common courtesy to shut the door when taking a piss? And was she supposed to hand him the file folder with his talking points while he had his hand on his little wee-wee, taking a wee-wee? And how could she do that without looking at it? It was gross enough that he'd tried plenty of times to interest her in said wee-wee. Blech. He was old and ugly. Nothing about that man's penis would ever come in contact with her. She'd opt for celibacy at the top of a barren, wintry, dystopian wasteland of a mountain in Siberia (are there mountains in Siberia?) instead.

He reached his free hand behind him, demanding his papers. "Hurry up, I don't have time to waste."

Evidently not if he was still urinating. She wanted to see how he'd get the papers out of the folder one-handed.

Instead, he finished peeing and zipped up, not even bothering to flush or wash his hands as he grabbed the talking points. "Come on, you're making me late." How, precisely, his urinating was her fault in making them late was a mystery. Gaslighting bastard.

14

Meanwhile, she made a mental note not to let her hands, or any part of her entire being, come in contact with anything his germ-laden fingers had touched, ever.

The debate was being held at a network studio about three blocks away. Normal people would walk there on such a pristine, sunny early autumn day, but instead his driver was at the ready to hasten them off.

They popped into the car, raced the three blocks to the studio, the driver opened the senator's door — so much for chivalry — leaving Meghan to scurry after him like an abused dog seeking the attention of her cruel owner. A handler named Janie from the studio greeted the senator and didn't even bother with Meghan as she led them to an elevator. The senator greeted the woman by clutching her torso (hand precariously edging her boob) and kissing her on the lips, so deeply inappropriate on so many levels. Meghan was hoping his lips were as disgustingly filthy as his hands were.

They took the elevator to the eighth floor and got out.

As they walked down the hallway toward the studio, Janie filled the senator in on timing. "Congressman Tanner is already in there with his aid waiting on you, sir," she said.

"Tell Tanner he can go fuck himself if he's going to play nasty," the senator said as Meghan elbowed him in the ribs, reminding him that speaking to members of the media in that way was not conducive to the best coverage. Although considering Janie allowed him to touch her lips with his — *can you even imagine?* — maybe it was irrelevant what he said or did in her presence.

As they entered the studio, Deborah Mott, the anchor who would be moderating the debate stepped forward. "Senator DeLallo! So lovely to see you again!" she reached forward to shake his hand, the one he'd just had on his gross, germy Johnson not twenty minutes ago, and he pulled her in and kissed her on the cheek. Manhandling a woman against her will was a skill he'd mastered long ago. "Looking good, Debbie baby." He pinched her butt. Meghan wished she could fade into the darkness that enveloped the outer ring of the cold studio. Instead, Deborah escorted them toward the empty dais. DeLallo's challenger, Congressman Tanner, a boyish thirty-something military veteran with dimples and a golden boy smile, stood erect and waiting. Meghan wondered why she couldn't work for someone so easy on the eyes, rather than her boss, who looked much like those large rodents you see dragging a slice of pizza down the steps of Penn Station on YouTube.

"Senator, I'm sure you've met Congressman Tanner," Deborah said. "And this is his new press secretary, Kirby McCaffrey."

Meghan's ears perked up and she knit her brow. Kirby. How many press secretaries named Kirby were in this town? She strained to look past her boss, past the anchor woman, past the congressman, past her brain-throbbing hangover, and there she saw him, in all his still-hot glory. Well, fuck. Of all the guys she could have cock-teased and made out with in this town, it had to be him?

"Meghan?" he said a bit too loud. Meaghan pretended she was busy with papers she was perusing. "Meghan? Is that you?"

"Who's Meghan?" his boss asked him.

"Over there," he said, pointing straight at her. "That's the woman I told you I was making out with at the bar last night."

Jesus H. Christ on a popsicle stick. Really? Who tells their boss that sort of thing?

"Remember I told you about the gorgeous woman? But she wouldn't give me her number? But here she is—"

"You were banging the enemy?"

Meghan blanched, but the rest of what he said faded away immediately, because the mercurial Senator Antonio DeLallo, the man whose capricious temper could swing wilder than a menopausal woman's thermostat in a heat wave, turned to Meghan, flames practically licking from his beady black eyes. "You fucked Tanner's press guy? After what he said yesterday? Is there something wrong with you? You can't just keep your panties on, you just meet someone in a bar and the next thing you know you've got your hands on his cock?"

Count to ten, Meghan. Count to ten. She bit her lip and began to dig her fingers into her palms one at a time: One. Two. Three. Four. Five. Six —

"You're fired! And don't even bother returning to the office for your things."

"But senator, you don't know what you're talking about."

"I heard all I needed to hear," he said. "I'm not good enough for you, but this little fairy boy is fine enough for you to have sex with?"

"I didn't have sex with *anyone*. Please. Stop this craziness and I can explain!" As much as she hated the guy, she needed the income. She needed the job. Her whole uptight identity was wrapped up in it.

"Out!" His face had turned red and the pronounced veins in his neck and barren temples bulged alarmingly as he pointed at her. She'd witnessed this kind of rage in him before. It was almost a form of foreplay for him. When he wanted to impress women in his company, he always screamed at staffers and intentionally humiliated them. He must've thought Deborah would find it a turn-on. Highly unlikely. He looked like a feral honey badger in heat. Ain't nothing sexy about that. Meghan was just grateful he had nothing breakable within reach to lob at her, because practically the first stage of his rage was hurling heavy, fragile objects against the nearest wall. Meghan was well-acquainted with the sound of shattering glass, having witnessed him propelling paper weights, crystal U.S. Senate bourbon tumblers, mobile phones, even a set of bookends.

But Meghan knew there was no placating him. When his fury became volcanic, the eruption would continue and there would be no reasoning with him. It was like a rage orgasm. His poor driver would be stuck trying to talk him off the ledge. Either which way, Meghan knew she was officially jobless. Thanks to that loud-mouthed piece of shit dick-head she stupidly flirted with last night.

She turned to Kirby. "Admit it: I was right. All men are assholes. This includes that guy," she pointed at her now ex-boss, "and that one," she pointed at the congressman, then turned to him and nodded. "And most of all, you."

Chapter Four

Two Years Later

KIRBY woke to a loud buzzing sound, his right cheek pressed to his computer keyboard, the bright fluorescent lights above jarring him even further awake. With no windows to the outside world from here, he didn't even know if it was day or night. Just that he'd passed out at work. Again.

"The Senator wants you *now*," came a detached voice from the in-office intercom.

"Be right there." Kirby glanced at his watch: four in the morning. He'd been stuck at work because some stupid Senator had decided to filibuster a bill by reading *War and Peace* for the past seven hours. Kirby had to stay until there was some movement because it was a bill his boss had co-sponsored that was being logjammed by that idiot who'd been blathering aloud on the floor of the Senate since dinnertime.

What made Kirby angriest was that these senators didn't even represent convictions any more, but rather held their fingers to the wind to decide how best to fundraise; he felt certain they'd be all in favor of shitting on their own seat then sitting in it if it ensured reelection. He'd been working in Congress long enough to realize there was too much incentive to win (power, prestige, not to mention all the women you could wish for, lining up to sleep with you, even if you were ugly and old with a wrinkly butt sagging down to your knees; power was a bizarre and entirely mystifying aphrodisiac, apparently), and very little incentive to behave responsibly for the country. And one thing was for sure: he hated that too many members of Congress wouldn't simply compromise on anything anymore, and everything had to be a damned fight. One that meant poor Kirby never had a social life, never got to the gym any more, never enjoyed any personal time — even his meals out were with the Senator and a variety of lobbyists. Some people got off on that sort of access. Kirby would've rather been home watching TV with his dog. If he had a dog. But he couldn't, because who could have a dog with a life like his? He couldn't even keep a damned hamster. Not that he'd ever want a pet rodent — it just wasn't his jam.

No one wanted his life. No one but maybe that woman he made out with at that bar — probably the last time he felt like his life bordered on having a social life, the night he randomly sucked face with that really pretty woman who taught him how to tie maraschino cherries with his tongue. Lot of good that skill did him when he was never around normal people to amuse them with his useless talent. And then to think he basically took the job she had, once his boss beat her boss in the election.

He rubbed his eyes with his fists, then traced the imprint of his computer keys along his cheek. He really needed to get a life. Maybe he'd start with something basic, like yoga. Something that wouldn't be too taxing on his out-of-shape body and might help him feel a little more centered, now that his life was officially totally out of whack.

He'd overheard one of the interns talking about this yoga instructor named Sunshine who was supposed to be excellent. He'd have to Google to find out where she was located. With any luck it would be close to work so he might even be able to sneak out of the office for an hour every now and then. Just to try to stay sane.

As if.

Kirby spent the next thirty minutes suffering through the Senator reaming him for failing to generate any media attention for his boss' efforts to advance the bill he'd co-sponsored, but after his chastisement in front of the chief of staff, the legislative director and the secretary, was finally freed to go home to bed. At five in the morning. Ugh. By then he was wide awake — who could sleep after the adrenaline rush of extensive public shaming? He couldn't believe that his boss had turned out to be such an asshole. When he researched the job, he seemed like a decent guy with decent beliefs. He never even met the senator during his job interviews, but rather was vetted through the HR head and the chief of staff. So, it had taken him by surprise that part of the job description really should have read "whipping boy for out-of-control fuckwad power freak." Maybe that chick was right: all men are assholes. Oh well. Kirby was going to have to do some serious life evaluating, soon. But in the meantime, he really needed to decompress and badly, so he quickly googled that yoga class and found that there was a sunrise class, not far from his home. If he raced home and got some appropriate clothes – alas, tennis shorts would have to do — he could get there just in time. His body craved some internal tranquility. Short of a couple of weeks on a beach in the

Caribbean, an hour of yoga would be just the ticket.

If Kirby was a cartoon character, or maybe Kramer in Seinfeld, he'd have skidded into the classroom for the class, he was running that late. As it was, he opened the door, which creaked loudly, a big no-no for yoga, disrupting peoples' quiet time. He was shocked to see how many people showed up for a ass-crack-of-dawn yoga class — the space was nearly filled with probably thirty people. Which wasn't such a bad thing — he could slip into the back of the classroom and be anonymous and no one would really pay any attention to him, which was always helpful when it came to some of those poses that required far greater flexibility than his body allowed him. He was totally fine lurking.

He didn't even have a yoga mat so he tiptoed over to the shelves with mats, straps, blocks and blankets and grabbed the needed supplies, of course knocking down some blocks in the process and making a clattering noise. Could he be louder?

He rolled out his mat gently, set his wallet and phone and water bottle against the wall directly behind him, and settled down in the very dim room with the rest of the class. The instructor — was her name Sunshine? Something weird like that — coached the class through a succession of deep breathing while they all lay on their backs.

Kirby was starting to get into it, breathing in through his nose and out through his mouth, taking those deep belly breaths that somehow manage to calm down even the most tightly wound humans (like him). The biggest danger for him was that he would fall asleep, and everyone's serenity would be pierced with his loud snores.

He was really enjoying her playlist — not the usual woo-woo yoga music but just kind of cool, chill tunes — as he breathed in through his nose, out through his mouth. He could feel his body loosening up, all that tension releasing. He was going to have to make a habit of attending this class. If he ever got a free moment again.

Sunshine had been talking them through breathing in her soothing voice and then the room only had the quiet background music wafting through it. Until suddenly the calm was disrupted by a loud buzzing. What the actual fuck?

People sat up and looked around, trying to find out who was responsible for the unwanted buzz-killing noise. Kirby wondered, too, what it was. Till he turned his head and saw out of the corner of his eye that it was his screen that was blinking while his phone buzzed like a swarm of killer bees ready to take down a victim. FUCKKKKKKKKKK.

Chapter Five

MEGHAN opened her eyes after her daily thirty-minute meditation, once again refreshed and ready to be her best self, all day, every day. She couldn't minimize the sort of can-do spirit that bolstered her after her daily meditation. It had a magical way of distilling all of life's crap into a little speck of dust, and that was a good thing. Especially compared to back when her life had turned into a flaming dung-heap of rotten manure, when her life imploded in a dizzying moment of *fuck-my-life* in graphic living color. The quietude that meditation gave her allowed her to release the anger and stress and bitterness. Even toward that jerk guy who told her boss they'd hooked up— *hooked up!* — the night before the debate. She could honestly say she forgave him and held no animosity toward him at this point.

For the first few days after it happened, she'd curled up in a ball on her sofa, binge-watching any reality show she could find in which people were more miserable than she was. She needed reassurance that there was a worse bottom to reach than the one she'd landed in. The good news, she'd learned, was that there were plenty of circles of Hell far more miserable than hers. Eventually her mom came down from Connecticut and ordered her out of her unbathed, dirty-haired stupor and helped pack her suitcase for a three-week mom-endorsed decompression at a yoga retreat in the

Caribbean. God bless mothers the world over for caring for their babies.

It was the best thing she could have done for her mind, body and soul, and an important reminder that she'd nearly lost her sense of self-worth working for DeLallo for three years, and had bizarrely grown to embrace his verbal abuse as acceptable behavior, it was so insidious. It took severing the umbilical cord for Meghan to realize that she'd been trapped in a seriously toxic relationship with her gaslighting, manipulative, venal, narcissistic boss and his vast cadre of enabling sycophants. And it had made her steadfast in her certainty that she never again wanted to be trapped in such a destructive work environment. She wanted to be her own boss.

The beauty of her escape to the tropical yoga retreat was that it launched her well on her way to yoga certification, so with the help of her kind parents, who helped her financially as she redirected her life plans, she'd made an about-face in every aspect of her life within six months. Then with her dad's handy woodworking skills, she turned the carriage house behind her rowhouse into small yoga studio.

With the extreme change in her lifestyle and the complete freedom she finally felt, Meghan decided to nickname herself Sunshine. Because she finally felt like her body radiated sunshine with how good she felt all the time. Healthy and happy and fit and Zen: Sunshine was the perfect name to manifest the new person she'd become.

Meghan slipped into the studio to prepare for her first

class of the day, the Sunshine Sunrise, feeling invigorated and ready to share her sense of serenity with her fellow practitioners. She double checked her supplies in the back of the room, then strategically positioned all of her candles and lit them, keeping the lights dimmed to help set the mood. Soon people began to filter into the room. This early class meant that very little conversation was happening; no one seemed to be too chatty at that hour. Instead, people unrolled their mats and got right to business, on their backs, eyes closed, practicing their breathing.

It was a pretty full class this morning, filled mostly with regulars — friends she'd known from living on Capitol Hill and fellow Hill colleagues who had become devotees of her class over the past year or so, which made her feel good.

She'd started the formal breathing intro to the class when in the back she could see one more person show up — it looked like someone she'd not seen in here before. Unfortunately, he wasn't the quietest of people, and every move he made seemed to resonate against the serenity of the room. With her Spotify playlist of soothing music and those calming flickering candles, Meghan had created a sanctuary away from the hustle and bustle of the outside world, so she wasn't thrilled when anyone introduced unwanted noise to disrupt the solitude.

Sure enough, he went back to get yoga supplies and fumbled in the dark, knocking down a stack of yoga blocks, which all thumped as they landed on the hardwood floor. Argh. But Meghan wasn't going to let that bother her. She didn't allow such things to get in the way of her uncluttered mind.

Finally, the guy settled down and joined the class as Meghan walked them through their breathing patterns. All good. She was just about to begin a few simple, integrated poses to warm up their bodies when she heard a loud buzzing noise. Like, from a phone. *In yoga class!* Who brought a phone into yoga class? At five thirty in the morning! What the hell?

The entire class was instantly pulled out of their solitude and many sat up in search of the culprit. Somehow Meghan's gut told her immediately who it was — the random guy who'd shown up late and unequipped. Of course, it was.

She cupped her hand to her forehead and looked to the back of the room, where the guy was fumbling in the dim light, apparently for his phone.

"Uh, no phones allowed in here," she said, trying to maintain her cool. "There was a sign on the door that all phones had to be turned off."

"But-but-but the Senate's in session," he said, his brow furrowed. "You don't understand: I have to be reachable."

She rolled her eyes and pitied the guy for his perverse devotion to that polluted lifestyle. She totally understood what a bunch of BS that was, for starters. But really, not honoring one simple rule for her class?

"I understand completely that the Senate is in session," she said, mentally counting to ten, trying very hard to not be that woman she used to be who would flip out the minute things went south. "Probably most people in this room understand the implications of that as well. But we honor one another with the gift of peace and quiet, so I will ask you to please turn off your phone immediately."

"How about instead of vibrate I put it on silent," he said, holding his phone up as if to prove it was harmless.

She shook her head vigorously. "Sorry. Please turn it off completely. Even a phone set to silent will flash light in here and distract people from their practice. I'm going to ask you once again to please turn off your phone or take yourself — and your phone — outside."

Hard to Get By

It was hard to make out any of his features so far from the back of the room, and with nothing but scattered candles flickering throughout. But she swore he looked familiar to her. She just couldn't put it all together and figure out why.

Finally, they got past the phone controversy and the series of sun and moon salutation postures, mountain pose, forward fold, vinyasa, and down dog.

She proceeded to move the class into standing and balancing poses, from warrior to crescent lunge, a wide legged forward fold, and tree pose (her favorite, as basic as it was). During balancing poses she strolled through the room, gently correcting postures, making sure people held a position properly. She noticed the guy in the back was all sorts of crooked with his crescent lunge so she slipped over to him and stood behind him, gently placing one hand on the base of his spine and the other on his hip to correct his positioning. Which was when she realized who he was. Kerwin? Curtsey? God, what was his name? Oh, yeah, Kirby. Stupid Kirby the jerk who ruined her career. Of course, he would have his damned phone on. Well, crap. *Senate in session, my ass*, she mentally grumbled.

Of all the yoga classes, in all the towns, in all the world, he walks into mine.

She closed her eyes against this grim reality and re-centered her mind, returning to the moment, blocking out the extraneous clutter in the form of that motherfucker ruining her class (not to mention her life), and walked with intention to the front of the room, directing the class back to the floor for the seated yoga sequence. From spinal twist to pigeon to forward fold, bridge, supine twists, and happy baby. She had to take care not to rush through it, anxious as she was to get this class over and done with. As daylight seeped into the room, she stared back at the class nuisance in the back of the room and couldn't help but see in his inevitably revealing upside down happy baby pose that the man was packing. Whoa — was that a delayed morning wood? Or was he just happy to see her?

The end of final Savasana couldn't come fast enough. She needed to get that dude out of her studio, never to be seen again. He was bad karma with a capital K. Even though she couldn't get that bulge in his shorts out of her mind. Jesus, it had been a long, long time since she'd been with a guy — she hadn't been with anyone since well before that dreaded night of the cherry stems and blue whale sex talk. She'd been busy working on herself, and didn't have time — or desire — to integrate a man into her life. It had been enough work for her to get her own shit together; adding a guy to the mix seemed like that would only complicate things too much. But it was impossible not to let her mind go there — she couldn't unsee that. Perhaps now was the time she needed to practice that mindfulness and get the guys cock out of her brain. Brain-block the cock. She laughed. Clearly, she needed to get a life other than work.

She shook her head back to the present and realized she needed to let these people get on with their day. She chimed her Tibetan cymbals to get the classes' attention.

"Slowly start to bring movement to your body," she said. "Roll onto your favorite side as you begin to sense energy flowing through your body. Gently press your hands on the mat and come up seated, with your eyes still closed."

She sat, cross-legged, pressing her hands together against her chest. "Thank you for sharing your love, light and energy with me today," she said. "I invite you to bow and give gratitude to your mind, body and breath for taking you through your practice, and the rest of the day. I hope to see you back tomorrow, bright and early. Namaste." She nodded her head to her chest as the class replied "Namaste."

People milled about for a few minutes, a couple of them asking about her playlist, another thanking her for helping to start out her day with positivity. That always made Meghan feel especially happy.

She focused her attention on those who were speaking to her but kept half an eye on the yoga poseur in the back of the room, counting the minutes till he left.

Soon the class filtered out of the classroom, and Meghan turned her attention to blowing out the candles, glad she was finally alone.

"Sunshine?" a voice said from nearby. She felt a tingle up her spine at the sound of his voice. She wasn't sure if it was out of fear or lust. She chose to ignore him and continue to extinguish candles. Soon she heard him puffing out some of the candles in the back of the room.

"Thanks — I'm good. I don't need your help," she said.

She could feel him stepping much closer to her and it made her nervous.

"What if I said maybe I need your help?"

She squinted. Why on earth would she even want to help him? Maybe because she was a different person now and didn't let things bother her like she used to? And because the old Meghan would have told him to go fuck himself but she was Sunshine Meghan so that meant she was going to be centered and gracious and non-judgmental? Ugh, it was times like this that she missed Old Meghan, cause telling this guy to fuck off would have been so much more gratifying.

Chapter Six

KIRBY could not believe he'd gotten a hard-on while Meghan was manipulating his pose. *A damned hard-on*, of all the things! Don't you have to actually go to bed and sleep in order get morning wood? Isn't that why it's called slumber lumber? There wasn't even any slumber involved.

Shit, that was no morning wood; that was a visceral response to that fucking gorgeous woman who he knew kissed like her life depended upon it. That was a full-out sausage sunrise, brought to him by Sunshine — *Sunshine?* What the what? — the yoga headmistress who was going to haunt his head for the rest of the day.

He couldn't let her escape his life yet again. But he also had no idea how he could even pique her curiosity, given how she's stormed out the last time they shared the same air space. Back then she seemed damned near ready to wind up and punch him one. He would prefer not to end his serenity-inducing yoga class with a shiner. But this woman also didn't send off those stressful vibrations like the Meghan he'd met before. She seemed to be calm and chill now, and not the type who would kick him in the balls. Thank you, Jesus, for tender mercies.

He was trying to strategize what to do, how to even face her to speak to her, considering the last time they were face to face things went to shit in a mighty fashion. It didn't help matters that she was going on about her business as if he weren't the only person left in the room. While he pondered his options while also desperate to grab a little sleep before having to get back to work, he decided to help her blow out her candles at least.

"Sunshine?" he asked, curious about the name change thing.

When that elicited no response, he kept trying. *She didn't need his help, yada yada yada.* Of course, she didn't. The last thing she needed was the company of the guy who helped her lose her job. Which helped him eventually land said gig, for the opponent, that is. She probably wanted to punch him in the throat.

"What if I told you I need your help."

He surprised even himself with that line. Was he for real? Or just trying to pave the way toward an "in"? Cause "in" was where he'd have loved to have found himself with her, those many months ago as she kissed him with a frenzied fervor after that insanely seductive cherry stem-tying exercise of foreplay. He'd like nothing more than to be in her. But that wasn't in the forecast for the near, uh, millenium. So, if banging the babe wasn't on the menu, what was his motivation? What were his intentions? And as he thought about it, he realized that perhaps this was an admission. He'd been floundering for a while, really just surviving. Maybe she could help him feel like he still had a soul, since it had kind of felt as if it had been sucked right out of him over the past two years.

She squinted at him, super suspicious looking. "What do I have that you need? That you didn't already take."

He frowned. "Touchè."

She gritted her teeth and shook her head. "I'm sorry. That was the old me talking. I didn't mean that."

"It's fine. I deserved that."

She put her hands on her hips and faced him. "So, what is it that you need that I can provide?"

He leaned against the wall and heaved a sigh. "Maybe this?" He motioned to the room, as if the room was the answer to his prayers.

"And by this you mean?"

"Peace of mind? Calm? Serenity? Something other than whatever the hell it is I'm currently filled with but seemed to have temporarily tamped down while in your class?"

"So you want my studio?"

He rolled his eyes. "While it is a perfectly lovely studio, no, I do not want to take away your personal property."

"I guess that's a win for me."

"Again, with the burn." He pursed his lips and squinched his face.

Meghan pulled at her hair. "Argh. I regressed. Again. Disregard that." She had no idea the temptation to return to her old ways would ever present itself to her so suddenly and unexpectedly. And so aggressively. And here she thought she'd given up on her bad habits. What good would it do her to harbor anger toward this man who she hardly knew? Who she swapped spit with in a dark corner of a seedy bar. Who kissed like he had a PhD in kissing. Who, if this morning's evidence was any indicator, packed some powerful presence, downtown, that is. Where it mattered. Not that Meghan dwelled on things like that but damn, she'd been in quite the dry spell lately. And not that she slept around a ton — she'd spent too much of her adult years entrenched with working for Satan to have time for fun — but she had enjoyed dallying with a few men, enough to realize that size *did* matter.

Which started her thinking about how much better it would be to make love, not war. Um, not really make love — she barely knew the guy! Except that he ruined her life, the bastard.

Gah! Stop with the negativity, ~~Meghan~~. Sunshine.

She started mentally dialing through her affirmations, the ones she recited in her mind each morning: you are kind, you are loving, you are smart, you are calm. ~~You are not going to want to kill this jerk for stealing your job, ruining your life, then ruining your sunrise yoga class with his annoying Type A existence.~~ You are kind, you are loving, you are smart, you are calm. You are kind, you are loving, you are smart, you are calm.

Okay, she needed a plan of action. This was just a huge challenge to the new and improved Meghan — make that *Sunshine* — to walk the walk, not just talk the talk. If she could actually not just deal with this guy — the good kisser with the package, who no doubt had some sort of positive personality attributes — not the traitorous man she presumed him to be, then this would prove to her — not that she needed the proof, but clearly, she did if she was lapsing into her old jaded ways — that she was indeed a new woman. A new, improved version of who she had been. One who could suffer the slings and arrows that life would throw at her, and be stronger and more determined than ever to be the best she could be.

She would take on this guy — was it Kevin? Kenneth? Kamden? Nah — that's with a "C". Please. If you spell Kamden with a "K" you need to go back to baby-naming school. Maybe it was Keanu? *Ha! Keanu. That man cannot act to save his soul. And yet he gets all the best roles! What is up with that?*

Okay Sunshine, focus, girl. What the heck is the name of the guy whose name begins with K? *Kirby!* That must be it. Kick him to the Kirby. No, Sunshine, we will not think negative thoughts about Kirby the kisser with the big package. She was going to take on Kirby as penance of sorts. Or as a challenge to herself, to prove that she was who she claimed she was: a strong, independent, anger-free woman who was all about being her best self and helping others to do so as well. She was going to Sunshine-ize Kirby Whatever-his-Last-Name-Is. She made a mental note to look that up.

She stood up from the still smoking candle she'd recently extinguished, briefly relishing the wafting aroma of soothing vetiver, and faced her once-enemy, crossing her arms over her chest, and focusing her gaze on him. She could make him her project. From foe to friend. Ish. That might be a stretch. But she could be his mentor, help him discover there was more to life than suffering at the hands of a soulless piece of crap politician who uses people like toilet paper and is always at the ready to flush them in exchange for newer models. Kirby Whatever-His-Name-Is was going to be her project. Which of course meant she had to put out of her mind forever that kiss, and that package. Cause she could never be in that way with her mentee. That would be like those creepy teachers who sleep with their students. Nope. Nope. A thousand times nope.

Chapter Seven

KIRBY stood frozen in place, still trying to grasp why it was he'd just told this woman, who, to be real, was his nemesis, that he needed her. He'd not have chosen to be her enemy, but clearly, she loathed him, and probably with some good reason. From her perspective, he basically took her job. Even though that wasn't his intention.

Well, to a degree, it actually was, because he had been trying to help his boss get elected to ensure that her boss had to vacate the Senate seat. But that was before he knew she was *that* Meghan. Or Meghan was she. Whatever. That Meghan was the press secretary for the senator who he helped his boss boot out of office. And it was hardly his fault that Meghan got booted well in advance of even that.

Then again, it was sort of his fault. He'd stupidly blabbed his personal stuff to his boss, who'd then blurted it out in front of everyone at that TV station. But he never thought it would come back to bite him in the butt like it did. *What the heck?* He was just trying to sidle up to the guy, get a little chummy. After all, if he was to be his mouthpiece, didn't that mean he needed to be close to him, to have his finger on the pulse of the guy's modus operandi?

If only he knew then what he'd figured out pretty quickly: the Senator didn't give a shit about Kirby's dull life, unless he could somehow use it to exploit his own agenda.

Which was what he evidently chose to do that day at the debate. And for which he didn't even bother to apologize. Right then and there, Kirby should've walked away. He should've realized the guy was a flaming asshole. But he was still starry-eyed about working as a press secretary for this war hero guy who claimed to have beliefs that aligned with Kirby's. He'd soon learn that was a bunch of nonsense too; the senator's beliefs basically aligned with whomever was donating the most money to his campaign. Sometimes Kirby felt like a complete dolt for having believed the guy had a set of morals. What was it the jerk had said to him? "Morals are for sissies."

Kirby gave that a mental eyeroll. Sissies? *Really?* So, to be rooted in a belief system meant you were a weak loser? At least in his bosses' eyes. No wonder the past two years of Kirby's life had sucked. No wonder he was questioning his own moral compass (or fearing a lack thereof). He'd been suffering a veritable case of Stockholm Syndrome. Aligned himself with his captor, who gladly led him by the nose like the gullible schmuck Kirby had proven himself to be.

Christ, maybe he *did* need this woman's help. Meghan or Sunshine or Butternut Squash, whatever her name was. She exuded a sense of calm and chill that Kirby likely didn't even realize he needed, stat. Had she at one time been him, the Stockholm Syndrome victim, captive of an equally reprehensible politician? And if so, how did she free herself from the vice-like grip that seemed to be squeezing the air from his throat?

Sunshine turned toward Kirby and put her hands on her hips. "So, you think you need my help?" She squinted at him. "That's kind of a weird thing to hear from the guy who conveniently got me fired from a job that was my entire life. A job he wanted so badly he was obviously willing to do anything to get it."

He shook his head vigorously. "You have to know that I had no intention of getting you fired." He ran his fingers through his hair. "I mean, I didn't even know you. I didn't know you worked for your boss. Well, I mean of course you worked for your boss. Everyone works for their boss. But I didn't know he was your boss. That all just happened in a blur. We had that encounter the night before, and then you, of all people, showed up at the debate. It was so sudden and so unexpected and so confusing and so—"

"Shitty."

He rolled his eyes. "You could say that."

"I actually did say that."

"Look, Meghan, you were right to say that. It was shitty. And I'm sorry it happened that way. It went from zero to sixty so quickly and then the Senator was flipping out on you and you left so suddenly and I didn't know you, didn't know how to find you, plus I was busy managing my boss. Who, by the way, I thought was a decent guy back then. But who I realize now is your typical sleazebag politician who chews people up and spits them out with regularity."

Sunshine lifted a brow. "If we are to continue this discussion, you'll need to refer to me by my chosen name, Sunshine."

He squinted his eyes. "You mean that's not just a business name, like a 'Sunshine's Bar & Grill' thing, only you're actually Meghan?"

She pursed her lips. "Meghan was a woman who was strung out on stress hormones, the Cortisol Queen, at the mercy of a pretty cruel employer who mastered the exploitation of his staff the way a lion tamer would subjugate a wild cat. Meghan had no coping tools to deal with the pressures of that job," she took in a deep breath, reminding herself that she was no longer living that life. "When I started over again, when I learned to take care of myself and treat myself with kindness and forgiveness, I became someone different, and chose my new name to reflect my outlook on life. I threw off the shackles of servitude that were holding me back. Now I'm my own boss, I carry the outlook that makes me feel good and I hope helps others to feel good. So, yeah, from now on, Sunshine it is."

"Does this mean we can get back to where we started? With blue whale sex and erotic cherry stem tying with our tongues and making out in a dark corner of a seedy bar?"

A guy could always hope, right?

"Uh, *hell* no," she said, wrinkling her nose. "Dude: know that this is going to be a purely transactional proposition. You are my project, plain and simple. And as such you will be under my tutelage. And as such there will be no hanky-panky, no innuendos, no insinuations, nothing. Straight up, above board, teacher-student stuff. Besides which, what happened at that bar was a classic behavioral manifestation of Stressed-out Meghan, and I'm no longer that person that let professional pressure dictate her life. Which means you and me," she wagged her pointer finger at him and then at herself, "Are not, and will not ever be a thing. Ever. *Capisce?*"

Kirby heaved a sigh. How the hell was he going to straddle his Type-A day-job-from-hell with his newfound hobby of learning to chill the eff out courtesy of a woman he wanted nothing more than to get up close and personal with?

Chapter Eight

SUNSHINE was still reeling from this sudden turn of events. Despite living and working on the Hill, the last thing she ever expected was a confluence of lives past and present to intertwine in this manner. That guy, the cherry stem guy, of all people, to show up and be loud and intrusive in her morning class. Murphy's Law. Damned Murphy.

And now she somehow agreed to mentor him out of his hellscape existence. Now that she had experience with it. But for it to be him, of all people, she agreed to mentor, well, that seemed like a less than great idea. First off because he had a large degree of responsibility in spiraling her into the rock bottom where she marinated in misery for far too long. She surely didn't owe him this kindness. But then again, this should and would be Sunshine's jam. Help a fellow traveler, someone who is no doubt suffering from what she'd experienced firsthand. Professional and personal malaise due to a professionally abusive lifestyle. If she could turn her own life around, surely, she could help this guy out of the shitter as well. Added bonus points for taking on the enemy. Ish.

The big question would be this: how? How the hell was she going to do this with the guy she didn't even know, who she merely related to what had put him in such stressful situations. And if nothing else, surely, she was by now pretty damned good at excising that from a life.

Sunshine crossed her hands over her chest and lifted her left foot up against the inside of her right knee. A little modified tree pose. And she was going to have to be that tree, the solid, rooted, reliable person who could do this.

"I'm going to have to think about how to do all of this," she said, spreading her hands out as if there was some actual entity there that needed her help. "In the meantime, I want you back here at seven o'clock tonight for my sundown class."

Kirby blanched. "Seven o'clock? As in, when normal people are already off work for the night but people like me are pulling out a bag of Sour Patch Kids to gnaw on because we realize we are going to be stuck at work for at least two more hours and there will be no time to even order food?"

She pursed her lips and nodded, closing he eyes to figuratively close out the bad juju that wafted around this dude like the stench from a skunk. Sure, he was cute enough, but then again, so were skunks, and no way did you get anywhere near up close and personal with a skunk.

"Yep. Be on time or the deal's off. And make sure your phone is silenced. For that matter, make sure you eat something beforehand — I don't want your stomach growling, either." She motioned to her supply room. "You arrive on time, go in there and get your mat and blocks and stretch strap and don't forget the eye mask for final Shavasana. Set yourself up, be sure you have an arm's length distance between you and anyone else, as it's a crowded class. And then when we have begun our practice, you need to divorce yourself from the noise pollution in your brain and just be in the moment."

"While I wonder if my boss is going to fire me?"

Sunshine shrugged. "I would think you of all people would realize that not only will your boss eventually fire you, but it will end up being the best gift he could ever give you. You just aren't quite ready to receive it. Preparing you for that is my job now."

Kirby scowled. "I didn't say I wanted to get fired."

Sunshine crossed her arms over her chest and shook her head. "Can't you see how enslaved you are? Free yourself from the yoke of oppression that is your chosen career path. It's entirely your life to control."

"But what about my paycheck? I have a lease, a car, bills to pay."

"Trust in the process and it will all work out as it should."

Kirby looked like he might erupt into shouting. Or tears. It was a crapshoot which one. Either which way, that was his problem, not hers.

Instead, he repeatedly muttered "trust in the process" under his breath. And Sunshine thought she could faintly make out something to do with a cherry stem. She just rolled her eyes.

"We have a deal?" She extended her hand toward him.

Kirby paused for a minute, then slowly reached his hand to Sunshine, slipping his fingers between hers. His hand was warm, his fingers, well, inviting. Almost suggestive. Sunshine wasn't sure if she had just taken on the biggest challenge of her life, or created the biggest challenge for her to resist this man, who would forever be a big fat no-no in her world.

Chapter Nine

SLEEPLESS and bleary-eyed, Kirby barely had time to run home and shower and get back to work, then spent the day running interference for the senator with reporters wanting to know when his bill might move forward now that the filibuster had ended. At that point Kirby could have cared less about the bill. He was both counting the minutes till his sundown yoga class with Sunshine and dreading it, too. And wondering if he might just fall asleep during it. Wouldn't that be embarrassing, if he started snoring in the middle of it? It was entirely possible — he was that exhausted.

Luckily the Senate would be out of session after today, so he'd be able to catch up on sleep and life a little bit, finally. It was the only thing that kept him sane these days. He'd completely missed breakfast because of his bold diversion to yoga class, so by noon he was desperate for some nourishment, and slipped out to grab a bite in the cafeteria in the basement of his office building, where he ran into his friend Shelly Amaro, a fellow press secretary.

"Hey Kirbs, how's it going?" she said as she held her cup to the soda fountain machine and hit the ice button.

He shrugged. "You want the truth or should I smile and lie to you?"

She laughed. "Sweetie, we're burned-out gladiators in the same arena. I think it goes without saying that you're not kicking back and smoking a Camel every day."

"Yeah, also haven't had a chance to sit down and read the latest bestseller either."

"Or had dinner before ten o'clock." She frowned.

"Or breakfast at all."

"And how about being accustomed to life on the front line with a hotheaded politician who wouldn't think twice about throwing something at you if he was mad enough?"

Kirby rolled his eyes as he filled his jumbo cup with Dr. Pepper. "Been there, done that. Dodged the flying iPad."

"In that case, honey, you're lucky. I needed five stitches once when my boss lobbed a paperweight my way."

His eyes grew wide. "You're kidding, right?"

Shelly stuck out her leg and pointed to a scar on her calf.

"Do we have some sort of mental deficit that we continue to subject ourselves to such abuse so regularly? Whatever happened to that survival mechanism of fight or flight?"

His friend grabbed a bag of chips and tossed it on her tray as they joined the line to pay. "I think it's pure, unadulterated brainwashing at this point."

He shook his head. "I'll say." He grabbed for his wallet and paid for both of their meals.

"Thanks, Kirbs. I'll buy next time."

He waved his hand not to worry about that. "I think we go into this job so optimistic and childlike in our beliefs, like we can make a difference. And then it eventually morphs into death by a thousand papercuts, each day the grind of the job—"

"—and the fire-breathing of our bosses—" she scrunched her nose at the idea.

"It just chips away at our morale, at our self-esteem, at

our *joie de vivre*, whittling us down to a mere nub of a human."

"You have *joie de vivre*?" They grabbed a table and sat down to scarf down their food.

"I did. I think maybe when I was ten years old." He laughed.

"Yeah, there's not much joy circling around this place, is there?"

"Not gonna lie, the last time I felt happy was before my boss won the election. I mean even election night was so fraught with stress and anxiety, it was hard to be too elated. Plus, I knew what loomed before me at that point, with long hours, and irritable bosses who expect everything to go their way."

"Yeah, you guys had a tough campaign too. DeLallo was a junkyard dog."

Kirby used his teeth to open the foil packet of ketchup he'd grabbed at the condiments table and squeezed it onto his fries, then popped one into his mouth. "You don't know the half of it. Did I ever tell you about his press secretary?"

"That woman Meghan something or other?" she jabbed her fork into her salad, spearing lettuce into her mouth.

"One and the same," he said, taking a bite of his burger. "Did I ever tell you how I accidentally got her fired?"

"If you did, then you did her a favor. Working for him probably took a couple of years off her life."

"Yeah, well, I'm sure she'll never forgive me for it. But weirdly I ran into her today."

"Oh yeah?" Shelly took a sip of her soda. "Who's she working for."

"Herself."

"What? She ran for office?"

Kirby laughed. "Not hardly. It's weird. She quit the Hill

and became a yogi."

Shelly laughed. "That is preposterous. Did she have some sort of mental breakdown?"

"Hell if I know. I just know I stumbled into her yoga class this morning at dawn as I staggered home to get a few hours of shut-eye and now I have to try to make amends."

"And you'll do that how?"

"By letting her save me." He laughed. The idea that she could do any such thing was beyond comprehension. He took a long sip of his drink.

"Is this some sort of slang for a way for you to get down her pants?"

Kirby spluttered Dr. Pepper onto his lunch.

"What the hell makes you think that is even on the table?"

"Because I can see the dopey look in your eyes," Shelly said, popping a chip into her mouth, crunching hard for emphasis. "You're too transparent. So, you somehow got this chick fired, she hated you for it, and now you're going to let her save you — god knows how — so that you can bang her?"

"Jesus, Shelly, you've been at this too long. Your cynicism has turned your soul to ice."

Shelly laughed. "Stick with me, kid, you'll learn a lot."

"Apparently if I stick with her, I'll unlearn all of that."

Shelly shook her head. "If I was a betting woman, I'd place all my money on this being a hard fail. This job is near-impossible to leave. My boss likes to shit this line down my throat constantly: 'there's a line out the door of people who want your job. There are only a hundred of you in the country. Suck it up and suffer for it, baby.'"

Kirby sighed. Maybe Shelly was right. Maybe he was doomed to a life of misery at his own doing.

Chapter Ten

THAT little one-on-one with the maraschino cherry guy left Sunshine feeling a bit unnerved, off-balance. She'd been doing so well for so long but his mere presence dredged up feelings she didn't want to feel. About her former job, about her former boss, about him. And the feelings about him were complicated: it was hard to get over thinking what a grade-A primo jerk he was for having gotten her fired. But it was also hard to get over recollecting how much fun their little tête-à-tête was at Bottoms Up, what with the sexy banter and the hot kisses. Not to mention feeling his hard body pressed up against hers. It had been a long, damned time since she'd experienced anything hard with a man in immediate contact with her body. She sorta missed it. Not that she'd ever consider that with him. No, siree. That ship had sailed, cast away along with the knotted cherry stems she'd tossed on the floor of the bar (not that she made a habit of littering in bars, but to be real, it wasn't a place you frequented because of the cleanliness of the joint).

But if she ever were to consider hard bodies within close proximity of hers again, his seemed to be the only one of its kind she kept fantasizing about. Which was a problem, because she'd officially volunteered herself to save the guy. Not that she even knew what that meant, or how the hell she was going to do it. But she figured if she did it for herself, surely, she could lend her wisdom to someone more desperate than she to absorb it. And being a savior by definition eliminates one becoming a one-night stand, or fuck buddy, or whatever you wanna call it. Though that was kind of underestimating her abilities a bit — hopefully she could last with a guy longer than one night. She had dated that charmer Bryce for a long time. Till he decided her sorority sister was more his type. Though in hindsight she realized she was far better off without him: who needed a two-timing crap bucket for a boyfriend anyhow?

She decided to take a walk to clear her mind a bit and figured her neighbor James might want to join her, so she sent him a quick text.

"Meet me out front in two minutes? Don't forget to bring Pete!"

Pete was James' rescue mutt, a combination of Bassett hound, Labrador retriever and lord knew what else, evidently a product of a dog show hook-up. Sunshine laughed at the idea of a dog show one-night stand. Would that happen back behind the curtains, where the audience couldn't see the truth about the dog show? Or smack dab in the middle of the arena with the owners in their sensible shoes jogging across the Astroturf showing off the four-legged proof of their countless hours of toiling, only to have a rogue and horny dog charge the turf and mount that proud little Bassett hound. It wouldn't take but a minute for that to work its magic. She shook her head: males of all stripes were assholes. Even the four-legged kind. Except Pete.

She stood lost in thought in front of her neighbor's adorable white picket fence, happy to see Pete's loping face and dragging ears appear at the front door.

"Petey!" she squealed, her hands in the air, running to greet the dog. "Cutest little crazy mixed-up kid, I missed you!"

Petey jumped his stubby legs up onto Sunshine's knees, his tail thwapping his joy at seeing his friend. Sunshine handed him a cookie, which he swallowed whole.

"How many times do I tell you Petey's going to turn into a watermelon if you keep giving him cookies all the time?"

Sunshine thrust her lower lip out. "But auntie Sunshine loves to love on Pete!" She gave James a hug. "Besides, food is my love language."

Her friend swatted her on the arm. "No kidding! Me too! Which is why Pete's getting fat."

They took off walking toward a nearby dog park.

"And why you cook the most amazing meals for Luke every night."

"Not gonna lie — I do the cooking because Luke's such a mess in the kitchen."

"You mean it's not because you show your love with food?"

"It's because I show my hatred for washing dishes!" James laughed at his own joke. "But seriously, you're right, I do love to smother him with love and in my case that usually involves lemon risotto and some fresh tuna steaks from Maine Avenue."

"And knowing you you'll probably be making him chocolate souffles for dessert."

"Did that last week."

Sunshine rolled her eyes. "Why can't I get a hot-looking guy whose love language is food and who knows how to actually cook it?"

He smiled at her. "Any time you want to join us for dinner, say the word. We'd love to have you."

"Aww, you're too kind," she said, rubbing her stomach.

"Though now that you mention it, I haven't got dinner plans for, oh, the next ever."

When we get back from our walk you can take a look at your calendar and we'll settle on a night for you to come over. Deal?"

She rolled her eyes. "You don't have to ask me twice! I'll be more than glad to show up. I'll bring a bottle of wine."

"Perfect."

They got to the park and James unhooked his dog and handed Sunshine the Chuck-it wand to throw a ball. "Have at it, my friend."

Sunshine tossed the ball for Pete to retrieve till the dog gave up and plopped on the ground, the ball nestled between his from legs, secure from rogue thieving dogs.

"What is up with dogs doing that?" she said.

James shook his head. "I guess we all gotta grab hold of that little sumpin' sumpin' we can stake our claim on. What's your sumpin', Sunshine?"

She pursed her lips. "It's funny you say that. For so long it was just my dumb day job, where I was emotionally abused and grossly underpaid and overworked for years. It got so bad I almost took pride in it — like I was so tough I could withstand it all, because I was so meant to be doing that."

"It's easy to lose yourself to your work, for your whole identity to get wrapped up in it."

"But then it was the greatest thing in the world to divorce myself from it. I mean look at how much happier I am now." She held out her arms in wonderment. "I was such a cranky beyotch for so long."

Her friend arched a brow. "No comment."

She laughed. "It's okay, you can say it. I wasn't fun for me so I wasn't fun for anyone else either."

"But then you grabbed the bull by the proverbial horns—"

"And got my shit together finally."

"Lucky you — some folks never get that chance."

Yeah, well, you wanna know something weird? You remember the cherry stem guy?"

James sat down on a nearby park bench and motioned for Sunshine to join him. "How could I forget? Luke and I found you weeping on your porch stoop and spent hours trying to console you."

She shook her head. "Pathetic, right?"

He leaned down to pet Pete's head. "Not at all," he said. "You'd lost what you though was most important in your life. It made sense — you had to go through all of those stages of grief. But what about the cherry stem guy?"

"He showed up in my class this morning."

James gave her a gentle smack to her arm. "Get out of here! That must've taken some nerve of him after all he did to you."

Sunshine rolled her eyes. "Are you kidding? He had no idea it was my class. And good lord, he was a hot mess. Showed up all disorganized and thought he could have his phone on — in a damned yoga class! — and he made all this noise and, honestly it was pitiful. So pitiful that when he started begging me to help him, I relented and agreed to."

James squinted at her. "Help him do what?"

"I don't know what the official term is. To get his shit together?" She shrugged. "He seemed so pathetic and sad and stressed and just a total mess. And then he basically admitted it and asked for help."

"And you agreed?"

She knit her brows. "I know, right? How weird is that? The guy who took my life away from me—"

"Who you might also say is the guy who gave your life back to you."

"Huh." She frowned. "That's not entirely inaccurate."

"Perspective, my dear," he said as he tapped her nose with the tip of his finger. "So, you're going to teach him how to Zen out and stop being an uptight slave to a shitty boss?"

"An impossible task, isn't it?"

"If anyone is capable of it, you're the woman for the job."

Sunshine kicked her toes at the pebbled walkway in front of where they were sitting. "But it's weird, don't you think? I mean I hated the guy and—"

"—you lusted after the guy before you hated him though."

She grimaced. "I'm sorry, but '*lusted after him*'?" I think not.

"Wanted to jump his bones?" He smiled.

"Have you *ever* known me to be a bone-jumper?"

He slapped his knees. "Did you hear that, Pete? Sunshine's trying out for the comic circuit next."

"I'm serious!"

"Did you or did you not make out with the guy — a complete stranger, mind you — in the dark recesses of that stanky bar?"

She thrust out her lower lip. "Yeah, but that's different."

"In what way?"

"I mean I wasn't about to jump his bones!"

"If you didn't have crazy work demands the next day, would it have been possible that you might have taken him home for a little, uh, maraschino stem-tying tutorial?"

She squeezed her eyes shut. She knew deep down that maybe, just maybe, that was a distinct possibility. She'd been in such a bad space, was still smarting from that jerk Bryce. She was lonely.

"Gah!" she threw her hands up. "I don't know. Maybe. But that was then, this is now."

"Now you're his little guiding light, showing him the way out of the dark."

"Yes!" Her eyes popped open. "Precisely!"

"And while you're at it maybe you can get a little sumpin' sumpin' on the side."

"No!" she shook her head with a bit too much fervor. "That would be unethical."

"You mean according to the '*Beginner's Guide to Rehabbing Neurotic Dudes* handbook'?" He whistled for Pete as he laughed.

Sunshine glared at home. "Are you mocking me?"

He shimmied pretend pom-poms in the air. "I'm your cheerleader, honey. Just trying to get Sunshine a little action."

"Action is overrated."

He chuckled. "Says the woman who hasn't seen any since the Pleistocene era."

"I'm not *that* old."

"Figuratively speaking." He stroked his dog's head as he continued. "My advice to you, dear Sunshine, is this: ride the horse in the direction its galloping. And ride that horse bareback." He poked her in the ribs with his elbow.

She rolled her eyes. Something in her gut told her he was far more right than she cared to admit. Nevertheless, who was Sunshine to listen to sage advice?

Chapter Eleven

KIRBY'S pulse skyrocketed as he clock-watched, knowing that he was going to have to pull some tricky maneuvers to slip out of the office before midnight in order to get to Sunshine's sundown class. He could feel his heart racing, along with a crazy need to breathe into a paper bag to avoid passing out from hyperventilating. Jesus, when did he become such a pussy, scared of his damned boss like a cowering little mouse at the sight of a towering cat? And wasn't that it, frankly, that his bully boss thwapped him around with his fat paw and extended claws and battered his little mouse self around with a perverse sense of joy? When did his spine turn to mush?

He weighed his options as the clock neared quarter to seven: be honest and tell his chief of staff and boss he had to leave early for a prior commitment, or just slip out and hope no one missed him. In keeping with his current modus operandi, he opted for the coward's choice: he quietly exited the office, surreptitiously glancing behind him the entire way out of the building until he'd cleared the block. He practically expected they'd send the Capitol police after him for his transgression. Imagine — leaving work in the evening like normal people! The nerve!

Of course, waiting that long to leave meant he had nothing to change into for class; he was going to have to hope for the best in his suit pants and button down. He'd just remove the tie, roll up the sleeves. And he'd have to take off the wing-tip shoes. Surely others had practiced yoga in something less user-friendly. In a normal world, were he to leave work at a reasonable hour, he'd be grabbing something to eat right now. Unfortunately, that meant his stomach was going to be growling all through class. He just hoped it was only his stomach that would be raging at him, and not his telephone full of sound and fury from the senator.

He intentionally waited until about thirty seconds till class to enter. He wanted — no, *needed* — to be hidden in the back, away from real yogi-types who would cringe if they had to see him in action. And hopefully to avoid Sunshine coming around touching him again like she'd done this morning. That would be seriously contraindicated due to his unforgiving suit pants.

Thankfully the lights were already dimmed by the time he took his place in the far back corner. The woman on the mat closest to him looked at him like he was nuts for wearing his work clothes. He was going to pretend he was just really dedicated to the cause.

As Sunshine guided her class through sun salutations and downward dog, Kirby hoped he might warm up just a little bit, maybe not feel like an aged oak tree unable to bend to the wind. But no, he could barely hold his down dog pose, made even harder with his suit pants restricting his movement.

Halfway through class Sunshine directed the group to do some damned forward bend with legs spread wide and naturally that's when she made it to the back of the classroom to correct poses. Kirby's sock-clad feet started to slip on the mat as he bent forward, causing his legs to splay even wider apart, and just when Sunshine approached him he felt a loud rip as the crotch seam of his pants split from back to front. Thank God he hadn't gone commando today.

He swore he heard Sunshine snicker as she placed her hands gently on his spine and abdomen to straighten him out. There was no way she couldn't see that he'd ripped his damned drawers. On his good suit, too. Life just didn't get any better than this.

As class drew to a close, he thanked the heavens above for final savasana, if only because he could hide the embarrassing tear in his pants for five minutes.

As class drew to a close, the word *Namaste* was barely out of his mouth when he hightailed it to his pile behind him with his briefcase and overcoat to cover the evidence. At least he wouldn't look like too much of a doofus with his coat on.

"Dude," the woman who'd been next to him said as she rolled up her mat. "It's a lot easier to practice yogs in clothes that stretch." She winked at him.

He rolled his eyes. *No shit, Sherlock.*

Although he told himself he deserved that.

He was hoping to slip out of class unnoticed but Sunshine pulled on the belt of his overcoat.

"Not so fast, sport," she said.

He pointed at himself, pretending he didn't know what she wanted from him. "Me?"

She squinted. "Yeah, you. In the entirely inappropriate yoga pants."

He could feel his face turning red. "I know, I know. I get it: I don't own yoga-adjacent clothing. I realized too late that it was this or nothing."

"Your pants look like they were heading toward nothing." She laughed.

He shook his head. "I'm just striking out all over the

place with you, aren't I?"

She shrugged. "Oh, I dunno. You've almost turned the corner from unbearable to mildly amusing."

"Progress in the right direction?" He cocked an eyebrow.

She shook her head. "Probably not, so don't get your hopes up." She checked her watch. "But you're in luck. I'm willing to let you in on a little secret side-hustle I've been incubating. Maybe we can outfit you in something that won't be nearly as mortifying as this—" she waved her hand along his outfit.

Kirby knew he was caught between the devil and the deep blue sea. His choice was to return to work and hope the Senator didn't tear him a new one — which would go perfectly with his shredded pants — or to ignore his screaming paycheck in favor of the siren call of Sunshine Ferguson.

He reached into his pocket and checked to be sure the sound was still turned off of his phone. There was a good chance the thing might just spontaneously combust in his pants, which would be par for the course, but it didn't matter: he'd thrown in with the siren.

Ultimately it was no choice at all.

Chapter Twelve

SUNSHINE sometimes wondered why she was such a sucker. She could easily have told this guy to get out, he wasn't taking things seriously, she didn't have time in her life for his nonsense. But for some reason she felt the need to perpetuate his misery — revenge, maybe? Or just to fuck with him a little? Or maybe she felt a little sorry for him because she saw Old Meghan in him and felt some obligation to rescue him from that awful fate-worse-than-death to which he was doomed otherwise.

She heaved a sigh of surrender and crooked her finger at him as she opened the door of the studio and led Kirby to the back door of her cute little renovated rowhouse.

She pulled her coiled key holder off her wrist and slotted the key into the door, then led Kirby into a bright, cheery kitchen, which was painted a sunny yellow.

Kirby opened his eyes wide. "Good God, woman, you trying to blind me?"

"Ha ha," she said. "I tried to decorate my home the way my heart feels."

He pursed his lips, then frowned. "Wow, when you put it like that, I feel like a schmuck."

She shrugged. "Or maybe just a work in progress."

"Can I offer you a beer or a glass of wine?"

"I wouldn't say no to a beer," he said.

She opened the fridge and pulled out a bottle, popping the lid and handing it to him.

"Don't say I never gave you anything." She opened a bottle of red wine and poured herself a glass, then tipped her glass to his bottle. "Here's to — sheesh! I don't even know what to call this."

"You mean us, here? Being civil?"

She nodded.

"How about here's to new beginnings."

"I'll drink to that," she said as she tipped her glass to her lips. "And in deference to this newfound friendship, here's my first directive: take your pants off."

Kirby choked on his beer, as she let out a laugh.

"I knew that would get your attention. Come here." She reached for his hand and pulled him toward the living room and started to climb the steps. At the top of the steps to the right was a bedroom and to the left was a sewing room. "Pants off first, and I'll try to stitch up the seam, so you don't spend the evening with unwanted air conditioning down there." She pointed toward his crotch, and quickly noticed the telltale signs of arousal. She had no idea how she was going to manage this whole thing.

"Okayyyy…" Kirby said, slowly unfastening his belt, then unbuttoning and unzipping his suit pants. "As long as you're good with this, I'm good with this."

Sunshine didn't know what she was good with but she was taking James' advice and riding the horse in the direction it was galloping.

She grabbed his pants and sat down at her sewing machine. She threaded it with coordinating thread, then pinned the seams back together and ran them through the machine. She pulled the pants off, clipped the stray threads, and held the crotch up to the light to be sure she didn't miss anything. And took a surreptitious glance at Kirby in his white boxer-briefs that barely concealed what they were concealing. *Yowza.*

She handed him the pants. "Before you put them back on, though, this is what I wanted to show you."

She opened a closet door and pulled some men's yoga shorts and shirts from a shelf.

"My own brand. I've been whipping up prototypes in my spare time, with the plan to sell these once I figured out how to mass produce them." She tossed some in his lap. "See if something fits."

"You're a clothing designer, too?" Kirby's eyes grew large as he checked out the outfits.

"I've been sewing my whole life," she said. "I just started making my own yoga clothes because I was tired of paying Lululemon prices and knew I could make clothes I liked just as much."

Kirby stood up and unbuttoned his shirt, undid his cuffs, and shrugged out of his button-down, then tugged his undershirt over his head. And for a fleeting second Sunshine got to gape at what he'd been hiding underneath those boring work clothes. Broad pecs and tight abs and a sprinkling of hair across his chest. And that sexy hair under his armpits that made her want to run her fingers there. But oh, no, that was not a thing!

But to see Kirby in nothing but his boxer briefs was challenging her whole plan to remain detached. After all, hadn't it been ages since she'd been with a man? And to hell with whatever specious moral commitment she'd made to herself to keep the high road when it came to Kirby. Why? Who cared? Was there a band of morality police hovering nearby to ensure she not reach out and stroke his belly, right *there*, where that trail of hair was tempting her to do just that?

She no sooner entertained that verboten notion then he grabbed one of her tops and pulled it over his head and stepped into the coordinating shorts, which, to be real, were practically like wearing boxer briefs anyhow. Ideally no guy wants his junk flopping around while doing yoga poses. And seriously no girl wants to see it flapping in her line of vision, either. Except right now maybe she'd break that rule just a teensy bit.

He extended his arms out and turned, slowly. "You really know what you're doing, Miss Sunshine. These are so comfortable—"

"—and guaranteed not to rip." She laughed.

He shook his head. "Of all the dumb luck, can you believe that?"

She rolled her eyes as she reached over to tug on the shirt to see how it fit. "I couldn't believe you actually wore street clothes to class."

"My brain has been so overwrought with work for so long—"

"—You're preaching to the choir, my friend. I get it." She walked around behind him, pulling and tugging on bits of fabric, sizing up how it fit in the waist, the hips, the chest.

"It's all work, non-stop. No fun, no play, no—"

"None of this." She turned him toward her, then reached for the hem of his top, lifting it over his head.

In a million years she never thought she'd actually take James' advice, but now she couldn't imagine ignoring it.

Chapter Thirteen

IF there was the danger lurking of Kirby being objectified, he could hardly have given a care. Because right now he was having the most fun he'd had in years, just sipping a beer and chatting with a hot woman whose hands were on his body, maybe in a way he hadn't expected ever.

Sure, she was lifting his shirt over his head. And sure, those were her hands grazing his chest. And was she actually slipping her finger beneath the waistband of those yoga shorts, trying to peel them off? Or was he just imagining it? Or maybe she was just being helpful.

And if he wasn't mistaken — was he? — was this part of the rehabilitation of Kirby McCaffrey? Cause if so, he was totally down with it. This was the kind of reconstruction project he was totally up for. And one glance downward attested to his being up for it.

But what if he was misinterpreting her actions?

Just then Sunshine peeled his shorts — her shorts, really — all the way down his legs. And he realized he needed to have some skin in the game. He reached over and pulled the tie of Sunshine's yoga wrap, then deftly slipped it off first one shoulder then the other, leaving her standing in front of him in just a sports bra and skintight yoga leggings.

"If I knew this was what you meant by fixing me, I'd have done this ages ago," he said, reaching for her face with his hands and gently guiding her mouth to his.

Sunshine leaned forward and pressed her lips to his.

"This is decidedly not what I had in mind," she said, licking the seam of his lips, encouraging him to open his mouth. "But apparently James had other ideas."

Kirby leaned back. "James?"

She laughed. "Never mind. A pep talk from a neighbor."

They stood pressed together, just staring at each other. Kirby pulled the clip holding Sunshine's hair up, and it all came cascading down. He stood, breathless at his good fortune as he gazed into her azure eyes.

"I cannot tell you how many times I thought about that kiss, in that grungy bar," he said. "How badly I wanted to find you and recreate that moment. How bummed I was that my life turned in such a sour direction instead, all of my own doing."

"I'm not a big believer in do-overs," Sunshine said, her hands stroking along his bare back, "But I firmly believe in new beginnings." She grabbed his hand and pulled him toward the doorway. "But first, let's get out of here—this room is a major pin hazard."

She led him across the hallway to her bedroom, with a bed piled high with pillows and a fluffy down comforter.

She pulled him toward the bed, and again pressed her lips to his. Soon their tongues were twining, their breath hitching as they scrabbled to clutch at one another. Kirby thought he was dreaming, it was so unbelievable.

To think, a few hours ago he was worried about sneaking out of work. Now he couldn't care less if he ever went back to that office.

Sunshine traced a path with her tongue along Kirby's lips, down the column of his throat, pausing to nip playfully at his Adam's apple. She trailed her tongue to his chest, swirling it around first one nipple, then the other. She moved further south, licking a broad swath along that happy trail as she settled on her knees then slipped her fingers beneath the waistband of his boxer briefs and guided them off of him. She reached for his hard cock with both hands, drawing it to her mouth, and opened wide to take him all in, alternating sucking and licking till Kirby groaned with pleasure. With her hands on his ass, she pulled him toward her, helping to press his hot cock into her mouth even deeper.

But Kirby had other ideas and reluctantly pushed her off of him.

"I don't want to come yet," he said. "It's my turn to pleasure you. Finally. I've been waiting a long time for this."

Chapter Fourteen

FAR be it for Sunshine to turn down a man's offer to pleasure her. So, when Kirby scooched onto the bed and pulled her onto his lap, she wasn't about to turn him down. Especially with his huge cock pressed up against her, albeit with her yoga pants blocking the way.

Kirby lifted her long hair back over her shoulders, then slid his fingers beneath her sports bra and slipped it up over her head.

Kirby was a breast man through and through, and he couldn't help but stare at her gorgeous tits before settling his mouth over one fat nipple and sucking hard. Sunshine straddled Kirby and fed her breast to his mouth while she followed James' sage advice and began to ride Kirby's cock. The sensation of his mouth on her nipple while his fingers played with her other one, combined with her rubbing against his cock made her groan out loud.

"More," she said, and Kirby followed her orders, flipping her so that she was spread across the comforter, so that he could easily tug her leggings off, leaving her in a skimpy thong that she knew was drenched with desire.

Kirby moved down her body, peeling the thong down with him, and spread her legs wide. He looked up at her and she nodded. "Please." Her eyes were glazed over with lust. Damn, that James knew what he was talking about.

Sunshine felt shy as Kirby spread her pussy wide and admired it. But all it took was a long swipe of his tongue to forget about being bashful and she began to thrust her hips toward his face, urging him on as she moaned his name loudly. She hoped she didn't have any windows open or James would know for sure she'd taken his advice.

"Come for me, Sunshine," Kirby said as he swirled his tongue along her clit and slipped his fingers into her wet channel. "I want to feel your pussy squeeze against my fingers when you come."

She thrust once, then twice and felt the shards of orgasm splintering through her pelvis as she rode his mouth and his fingers to climax.

Jesus, how could she have gone so long without *that*?

Sunshine lay with her eyes closed as her heart rate settled down for a minute.

"Don't suppose you have anything, do you?" she heard Kirby say.

"Condoms?" Argh. Even if she had any laying around, they'd be long expired. "Normally I wouldn't be so foolish but I haven't been with anyone in years. What about you?"

"Trust me, the statute of limitations has run out on my failed sex life."

She winked at him. "Doesn't seem too failed right now."

He scooted up toward her. "But what about, you know?"

She smiled. "No worries. I've remained on birth control, so that's all good."

"In that case." Kirby spread her legs apart with his knees, notched his cock to her pussy and slowly slid into her swollen, wet channel. They both gasped at the sensation. "It's like you're custom-made for me."

Kirby held himself deep inside of her, grinding against Sunshine's pelvis, making sure she could feel him deep within her. Then he slowly withdrew and repeated, making Sunshine mad with pleasure. "Fuck, Kirby, I'm going to come again," she said as he stroked in and out of her, again and again till she fell apart at the sensation. Kirby thrust himself deeply inside of her again and stilled, releasing his come deep inside her pussy in pulse after warm pulse of his seed.

They soon fell asleep, their sweat-slickened bodies sated. At least temporarily.

Chapter Fifteen

KIRBY got up to pee sometime in the middle of the night and decided to check his phone. He'd left it switched to silent for the whole night. He dare not imagine what sort of implosions happened without him there to placate the senator.

When he looked at his messages he saw there were fifteen from the chief of staff, one more heated than the next. He played back a few of the voice messages until he got one directly from the senator — screaming in the background as the chief of staff held the phone, apparently.

"Don't even fucking dream of stepping foot in this office again, you good for nothing lout," his boss screamed at him.

So. He'd gotten himself fired. All for one good fuck.

He was trying to process how he felt about this. Did he feel relieved? Grateful? Stressed? Scared?

But the only thing he could think was that he needed to go back and join Sunshine in bed, to sink into her body and just feel all the feels that went with that.

He tiptoed back into the room but found Sunshine awake. "You okay?" she said as he laid down next to her.

He shrugged. "Depends what you mean by okay. If you mean am I cool that I got myself fired?" He grinned. "I have to say, I think I'm fucking elated."

She swirled her fingertip in his chest hair while leaning her head against his arm. "Huh. It's almost like I didn't even have to do any of the heavy lifting for you," she said, tapping his heart. "It seems it was all here just waiting for the right moment."

"But you know I think I'd be even more okay with things if I could maybe feel my hard cock in your wet pussy some more." He gave her a pretty please look, his eyebrows arched.

"Oh, you think so, do you?"

"I know so," he said as he lifted her up so she sat atop his cock and let herself slowly sink onto him.

"I'd say," she said, rotating her pelvis around his dick as she rubbed her clit against him, "that riding this horse in the direction it's going was some of the best advice I've ever gotten."

"Remind me to thank that neighbor of yours."

She smiled. "Maybe, but only after we get some more practice in."

She leaned forward and kissed him as she lifted and pressed onto his cock til he came in her.

And it was then that Kirby realized he'd found his Zen, jobless, but finally with the cherry stem-tying little vixen who'd made him crazy all those years ago.

Thank you!

Thank you so much for reading *Hard to Get By*! I hope you enjoyed it! If so, please help others find this book:

1. Help other people find this book by writing a review.

2. Sign up for my new releases email so you can find out about the next book as soon as it's available and get fun giveaways.
    http://eepurl.com/baaewn

3. Like my Facebook page.
    www.facebook.com/jennygardinerbooks

And I love to hear from readers! Let me know what you think about my books! You can write to me at jenny@jennygardiner.net, and visit me on the web at www.jennygardiner.net.

Are you new to my books? If so, you may love my popular *It's Reigning Men* series, starting with *Something in the Heir*.

He's a prince with a problem, she's a commoner with a getaway plan. Modern-day Prince Adrian of Monaforte has a most old-fashioned problem: his demanding mother wants him wed to her best friend's daughter, the hard-partying Serena. When his refusal falls on deaf ears, Adrian decides it's time for him to slip away from his gilded cage and figure out his life, all on his own. As luck would have it, event

Hard to Get By

photographer Emma Davison, weary of a revolving door of lost-cause men and tired of her outsider-looking-in career, is in need of her own escape clause, just in time to help a wayward prince in need. And she soon discovers that sometimes a girl's gotta sweep a prince off his feet. For any girl that's ever held out hope that some day her prince would come…or better yet, hoped that some day she'd come to him.

Read on for a taste of Something in the Heir!

SOMETHING IN THE HEIR

Chapter One

EMMA Davison had a date with a prince. Well, not really a date, but yes, really a prince. Calling it a date would be a bit of a stretch, considering she would only be within breathing distance of the man by dint of her professional skills. Emma had been hired to photograph His Royal Highness Crown Prince Adrian William Philip Nicholas Winchester-Westleigh, future King of Monaforte, in a series of grip-and-grins with wealthy donors at a Washington, DC charitable event. For Emma, this was a perfect night out with a man: one for which she'd get paid, and only for her skills. Professionally-speaking, that is. It was about as much of a pseudo date with a guy as she'd expected for the foreseeable future, since she'd sworn off men for a while after a series of dud relationships.

And while it was hard not to fleetingly fantasize about being swept off your feet by royalty, the fact was, those types of princes only came in fairy tales, and Emma wasn't a big subscriber to that sort of fiction. Having already tossed back into the swamp more than her share of warty toads over the years, she knew that at the end of the day, even a prince was just a man. And in her world, men hadn't exactly panned out. Besides, she'd seen the tabloids: this pretty boy was a player, a new woman on his arm in every city, rumor had it. As far as she was concerned, they could keep him. *Prince-schmince.* She sure wasn't looking for another love 'em and leave 'em type in her life. She was here to do a job, and the sooner she did it, the sooner she could go home and take a nice hot bath with a good book and a glass of red wine.

As she awaited the arrival of the guest of honor while hovering just inside the cordoned-off velvet rope section in the palatial Great Hall of the Library of Congress, Emma mentally ticked off the essentials she needed to keep in mind for the shoot. She'd thoroughly reviewed the protocol handbook with the palace's press secretary earlier in the week. All forty-six pages of it. She'd been told a curtsey would be a nice gesture, and warned not to shake the man's hand, which sort of seemed annoying, as if her own wasn't good enough or something. No vulgar language in his presence, which made her laugh, since under other circumstances she'd maybe have to show a bit of restraint in that area, but she figured she could refrain from an f-bomb for an hour or two.

Emma had actually practiced how to address the prince for a good while in advance of the event so that she wouldn't come across like a complete country bumpkin in his presence, repeating in front of the mirror, "*Pleased to meet you, sir*" till she could say it no more. She was ready. She'd even straightened her shoulder-length chestnut curls for the occasion, thinking straighter hair lent her a bit of gravitas. Yeah, she kept telling herself, she didn't care one bit about impressing even a prince.

She'd brought along her assistant and best friend Caroline McKenzie, whom she knew wouldn't screw up—though it was a crap shoot whether she'd hit on the man herself. Caroline, a green-eyed redhead with a penchant for serial flirtation, was known for her ability to pick up pretty much any guy she wanted without batting an eye. But Emma knew even she had her limits and would, with any luck, respect royal protocol, in deference to her friend's career.

Tonight Emma would remain on the VIP side of the

velvet rope as she set up to shoot the prince alongside all sorts of deep-pocketed D.C. dignitaries, with the President of the United States thrown in for good measure. Lately she'd found it hard to remain too starstruck in her line of work, shooting famous people as regularly as she did. But a prince *and* a president? As much as she wanted to play it cool, even she had to admit that was none too shabby.

Caro, standing just behind Emma, squealed in surprise when the prince's arrival was announced with blasts from those long royal trumpets draped with crimson flags bearing the Monaforte royal crest. It was straight out of a Disney movie when Prince Charming's arrival was heralded to the guests at the ball. As soon as the trumpets fell silent, a deep blue velvet curtain parted and the prince, followed by his right-hand man, stepped forward to the thunderous applause of the audience.

Emma was close enough to see that he had mesmerizing bright blue eyes. She was a sucker for blue eyes.

Just then a quartet struck up a tune and the music shattered her momentary reverie. She knew she had all of about two minutes to greet the prince and then get started with the host of images she needed to capture. There were titans of industry, political bigwigs and a collection of pandering celebrities already queued up, desperate for their own eight-by-ten glossy with famous royalty that they could mount on their wall like some taxidermied bear head. She had no time for gawking.

The prince walked slowly down the line, greeting one by one the organizers of the charitable event and members of the Monafortian embassy staff, all standing in the VIP zone near Emma. Everyone seemed to do a perfectly fine job with his or her allotted three seconds of undivided royal attention, making casual chitchat with the prince. Until it came to

Something in the Heir

Emma. Because as soon as the man approached her, she felt as if her tongue had become a sandbag weighted down in her mouth. And while a curtsey wasn't mandatory, it was what she'd planned on, until that very moment when her eyes made contact with his deep, sapphire ones, and she knew for certain she'd face-plant on his expensive royal bespoke Italian shoes if she dared try any tricky maneuvers.

Emma tried to give him a discreet once-over, but it felt awkward, like gawking at a stranger's tattoo, or trying to read the T-shirt message on the chest of a person walking by. She definitely wanted to avoid coming across like a sad-sack groupie, and had planned to play it cool. But then she found herself focused on his thick, wavy black hair, which led to a fleeting fantasy that involved burying her fingers in it while he was busily...*Oh, stop!* She tamped down that betraying thought, dismissing it as some stupid latent celebrity crush, all the while recognizing that her darned body was selling her out and swooning over the guy despite her strong inner protestations.

So when Prince Adrian stopped before her, bent his head down but raised his gaze and continued to fix it on Emma's eyes only, reaching both hands out for hers — totally defying that whole handbook of royal protocol — she simply stammered. And when he pressed his lips to the top of her hand, she could only gulp as she tried to clear what felt like a giant hairball lodged in her throat.

"Peas to greet you, slur," she said, failing miserably to just mouth correctly those five simple words, turning about fifty shades of red in the process. She felt certain she was going to be fired on the spot.

But instead of calling for his royal bodyguards to toss her out into the cold December night on the grounds of complete idiocy, he clasped her hand in both of his for a moment longer, his eyes continuing to hold hers, and smiled broadly. Emma could feel her heart beating in her throat, and she wondered for a minute if he was only holding onto her hands until someone else could grab them and haul her away. In handcuffs maybe.

"The pleasure is all mine. And please, call me Adrian," he said in what seemed barely a whisper, adding with a wink, "Oh, and by the way, I'm most pleased to greet you as well."

Emma was so glad she wasn't prone to throwing up because if she were, that would've been the unfortunate outcome of her moment in the spotlight with her "date." Instead she let him cling to her hand a second longer while she trembled just a bit and hoped to God her palms weren't sweating too badly.

The spell was broken when Caroline elbowed her, blurting out, and not in her inside voice, "Oh, my God. His accent is orgasmic. And did you get a look at that friend of his?"

Adrian and Emma's heads followed her friend's pointing finger, which led right to the tall, handsome brown-eyed blond man standing beside the prince.

"Who? Darcy?" Adrian said, waving his hand dismissively. "He's hardly anything to write home about!" He laughed as he gave him a friendly smack on the back.

"Don't listen to a word he says," Darcy said. "He's just jealous that women always choose me over him."

Which meant those women must have been certifiably insane, if they didn't want Adrian to keep for all eternity. Emma wondered if she could stuff him in her camera bag and no one would notice. And then she could have him all to herself. To join her in that bubble bath even. Which was an insane thought, considering she'd just met the man minutes ago. But he was obviously so good at charming the pants off of a girl, how could she not maybe at least ponder having her own pants charmed off, at least for a second or two?

By the time Emma snapped out of that delusional fantasy, the prince had finished greeting the receiving line and was engaged in conversation with some member of Congress. That was her cue to get to work, so she raised her camera up to her eye, her other hand turning the zoom on the lens to frame the shot, and started taking pictures.

A short while later, a syrupy-drawled senator approached and glad-handed the prince with a too-firm grip and slap on the back. So much for diplomatic decorum.

"You gonna tap that one?" he said to Adrian, his booming voice resonating. He nodded in Emma's direction, rubbing his paunchy belly like he'd had a satisfying meal, as she snapped the two of them in conversation. He might as well have been licking his chops like a starving dog. It wasn't the first time she'd been exposed to obnoxious good-old-boy comments from an old fogey politician. Such crassness seemed to be elevated to an art form in this town.

"You mean our lovely photographer?" the prince said, playing along. "Actually, she's the woman I'm going to marry." He gave her a wink, assuming she'd be complicit in his joke.

Instead Emma blanched, mortified that they were discussing her as if she was a slab of meat they were choosing off a hot grill, all for their boys-will-be-boys amusement.

"Yeah, in your dreams, buddy," she said in too loud of a voice as she continued to snap pictures, handily obscuring her face and thus her emotions. Her royal subject squinted his eyes at her and pouted, as if she'd hurt his feelings, and she immediately regretted her words. It made no sense to be annoyed with the prince; he was simply defusing the obnoxious comment made by the senator. But it was too late.

Within a minute he had his arm draped around the sexy trophy wife of a well-known lobbyist, and so Emma did what she always did to hide from the world and resumed snapping pictures.

"I'm so ready to get out of here," Caroline said as they sipped sparkling water while taking a five-minute break. "These old geezers around here with those gold-digging bimbos on their arms are giving me hives. Maybe I can kidnap blondie over there and make a run for it. Think his friend would notice?" Once again she pointed toward Darcy, who was dominating the conversation in a circle of women nearby.

They'd been notified by the event coordinator that the president would be arriving shortly, so Emma was taking advantage of a momentary break to run to the bathroom and double check that her equipment was ready for the big moment. Despite an encroaching sense of ennui about her job that had settled in recently, she was feeling anxious about shooting the president and wanted to be sure she got off all the shots she needed.

When she returned to Caroline's side, they worked their way back toward the front of the crowd to get in position for the president's arrival. She noticed how Caroline's gaze rarely left Darcy.

"Forget about him," Emma said, nodding toward the prince's assistant. "This place is crawling with Secret Service, at least until the president's gone. If you try to bag that one, you'd be hauled off for interrogation by Homeland Security, never to be heard from again."

Her friend shrugged. "You know, some of those Secret Service guys are pretty hot."

Something in the Heir

"You do know you've got a one-track mind, don't you?" Caro shook her head in dismay at her friend. "At least there's something going down my track. Ever since that last derailment with Richard what's-his-name, yours has been a whole lot of nothing. No train ever stops at your station."

"Please," Emma said, annoyance flickering in her hazel eyes. "I do not need to be reminded of that regrettable relationship. The jerk still owes me five hundred dollars I lent him. Not to mention my dignity, which he took off with along with that stripper from his buddy's bachelor party."

"Pretend I didn't even mention him," Caroline said, holding her hands up in defeat. "I totally forgot I promised I'd no longer resurrect your litany of painful break-up stories. At least not while at work. Although, you gotta admit," she said, wrinkling her nose as she held back her laughter, "it was sort of funny to watch him on YouTube jamming fifties in her g-string. Just think how romantic it is that one day they'll be able to show their grandchildren the video of the very moment they met."

Emma made a grumbling sound. "At least I figured out where my money went."

"And it was money well spent, darlin', if it meant finding out the truth about that one. Way cheaper than alimony."

"Which I'd have had to pay since he couldn't keep a job for more than six months." Sometimes Emma wished there was a punching bag nearby, just to get out her aggression toward the loser.

Their conversation was interrupted by the unmistakable sound of drums and bugles that precede "Hail to the Chief." Emma snapped one wide shot of an audience's worth of hands raised in the air, smart phones at the ready for their very own money shot with the president.

The president parted the velvet curtains, waved to the

crowd, then greeted the prince and his entourage while Emma clicked away on her camera. After a brief, five-minute address, he was whisked away by a coterie of security guards, *tout de suite*.

Once the headliner was gone, the crowd began to dissipate. Emma managed to pop off a handful of shots with other guests and the prince, and finally the embassy press secretary thanked Emma for her service and dismissed her.

She scoured the room in search of Caroline, who'd taken another bathroom break, just to let her know she was off the hook and could leave. She found her friend chatting up a cute bartender.

Emma tapped her on the shoulder, trying to draw her attention away from tall, dark and hottie, who seemed intent on slinging mixed drinks to impress, shaking cocktails atop his head like he was go-go dancer from the sixties

"I'd tell you that you can leave but it looks like you don't want to have a reason to slip out quite yet," she said.

Caroline startled and gasped. "You scared the crap out of me!"

"Just wanted you to know you're technically off-duty in exactly T minus ten seconds," Emma told her, pointing at the time on her cell phone. "Obviously you can feel free to stick around and latch onto some useless guy, but if I were you, considering the caliber of this crowd, at least I'd aim a little higher."

"Thanks for the sage advice, relationship expert that you are." She laughed at Emma. "But seriously, you know I'm not looking for the guy with the deepest pockets," Caroline said. "I'll take the hot bartender with the smooth moves any day," she said, pointing over to the guy pouring her drink, "— over some snooty, rich country club-type who wouldn't abide my less-than-uppity ways." She lifted the tip of her nose with her pointer finger as she said that, her long, straight red hair falling into her face.

Emma laughed and mussed her friend's hair. "Whatever. Have fun, and don't do anything I wouldn't do…"

"That leaves my options wide open," she said, holding her thumb and pointer finger up in an "L" shape to her chest. "How about just to prove you're not a complete loser, why don't you see if you can snare that cute prince and get your wild on?" Not that there was a chance of that anyhow, as the prince and his entourage had already taken their leave.

Emma fake-glared at her. "Thanks, but I'll take a pass on the Cinderella fantasy. Though he was pretty easy on the eyes. I'm surprised you didn't already commandeer that friend of his."

"Sadly, once I got finished wiping the drool from my chin, he'd disappeared."

"Leave it to you to not miss out on the eye candy, whether he's your basic bartender or a royal footman," Emma said, pausing to contemplate the thought. "Is that what you call them? Footmen? Do they do something with their feet, or have a creepy foot fetish? Sort of weird name, isn't it?"

"Probably more like henchman is my guess. Back in the day his footman would've cut off the enemy's head. Am I right? Ah, well, clearly we weren't born into that world, so I'm not gonna bother even fantasizing about it, not to mention decipher the terminology."

"Yep. Besides, imagine how high maintenance a prince would be. Sheesh!" Emma stuck out her pinky finger while pretending to pick up a delicate china teacup. "Spot of tea, Mummy? Oh, royal knave, fetch me my slippers!" she said with an exaggerated accent.

The two women practically fell over laughing, until

Caroline's mixologist cleared his throat at an elevated volume, trying to rein in his audience.

"Okay, then. Looks like Bartender Ben over there wants your undivided attention," she said, aiming her thumb over her shoulder at the guy. "I've got no shoots scheduled for the next week, which means I won't be requiring your assistance, so have fun mixing it up with this one."

Caroline's eyes grew wide and she mouthed "Shut up!" to Emma, then turned back to her man of the moment.

Emma took a final quick glance around the room as she packed up her camera bag. After working more hours than she cared to count with her feet wedged into a torturous pair of black stilettos, she wanted nothing more than to peel off her floor-length, black satin sheath, lose the strapless bra that was cutting off the circulation in her mid-section, and tug on her favorite oversized sweatshirt and yoga pants. Then she'd finally pour that very full glass of Chianti she'd been craving, and return to her natural slothdom.

The party was still going surprisingly strong, but since she was only contracted to do grip-and-grins of Prince Charming, there wasn't truly a reason to stick around much longer. Hell, she'd likely get pressed into service with the wait staff if she wasn't careful. Not like she had anyone she could hang around and chat with anyhow, with Caroline being preoccupied. That was the thing about her work world: being a worker bee at the ball wasn't really much fun, even if the top-tier champagne was flowing freely and the passed canapés probably bore a per-piece price tag that exceeded her daily meal budget.

For Emma, being an outsider at an insider's party was losing its luster; she was getting old enough to appreciate that it wasn't what it was cracked up to be. Sure, she got to share proximity with some of the world's elites, but since she wasn't a member of that rarified universe, it didn't rank a whole lot higher than being the one polishing the silver at the palace. It wasn't as if she could chat up the guests, comparing notes on their winter holidays in Aspen, shared vacations on Necker Island with Sir Richard Branson, or summering on Nantucket. The closest Emma got to summering (and when did that become a verb?) — not counting Caroline's annual skee-ball smackdown on the boardwalk in Ocean City, Maryland, which didn't quite elevate vacationing to the next level — was escaping to her parents' beach house in North Carolina every August.

Okay, she had to clarify this a bit: her job sure beat working in a windowless cubicle. And tonight's venue, The Great Hall, on a scale from one to wow, was no doubt a wow. Picture every little girl's fantasy of taking that Cinderella descent down a grand marble staircase, garbed in a luscious tulle ball gown twinkling with crystal beads, with the man of your dreams (like maybe that Adrian guy) waiting at the bottom to clasp your outstretched hand and pull you into an intimate dance. Throw in that two-story tall Christmas tree, which would put the famed Rockefeller Center version to shame on grandeur alone, and, well, this was where that dream would come to life. That is, if that was the kind of fairy tale you could somehow work out for yourself. Good luck there. Nevertheless, she attended interesting events, met fascinating subjects, and did so in some pretty spectacular venues. But for some reason this wasn't thrilling her the way it used to.

As Emma was working her way toward the coat check, she spied the obnoxious senator pawing at what looked to be a Capitol Hill intern, judging by the badge dangling from her neck. Emma quickly opened up her camera bag, pulled out her camera, and began snapping pictures of the senator in a clinch with the girl, his hand squeezing the young woman's butt.

"Hey, Senator," she shouted over the din of the crowd. "Wonder what your constituents would think about you tapping that."

She moved the camera away from her face and gave him a big thumbs-up as he quickly detached himself from the girl, who had to be fifty years his junior.

Gotcha.

With that, camera still slung over her shoulder, she grabbed her coat from the coat checker, handed the girl a buck, and slipped out a side door, never to be missed by those inside. Now to get back to the car, cross the bridge into Virginia, and be home in twenty-five minutes, tops.

Chapter Two

HIS Royal Highness Crown Prince Adrian was one very ticked-off man. He paced the floor of the private office-slash-holding room in which he was holed up as if he had somewhere to go. Only he didn't, since somehow his driver had yet to arrive to usher him back to the embassy. Although he might, soon enough, right on down the aisle, what with his mother force-feeding him a heaping helping of Lady Serena Elisabeth Montague, Duchess of Montague, like a fat spoonful of that disgusting, overpriced caviar that girl seemed to be on a steady diet of.

Despite Adrian's repeated entreaty to the contrary, his mother the queen had deemed Serena to be "ideal marrying material," via yet another text message to her son, and palace efforts were now under way to ensure the fulfillment of her wishes, regardless that they were in direct conflict with her son's own desires. Certainly it hadn't helped that Serena's mother, Lady Sarah, a close consort of the queen, had been touting the glories of her daughter to his mother for years now.

"*Serena Montague.*" He said, growling her name, swatting away his equerry and trusted confidante, Lord Darcy Squires-Thornton. "Despicable would be too generous a word to describe that manipulative witch. I'd no sooner wed that scheming, conniving—"

"Adrian," his aide said, stopping him with a hand against his chest and a stern look in his eyes. "The walls have ears."

Adrian glanced around the room, remembering that

there were indeed others nearby whose discretion wasn't guaranteed. It wasn't easy always having to worry that what you said could be broadcast publicly and not in a good way. Ridiculous, really. He was starting to feel almost imprisoned in his life of privilege, what with the extreme limitations on his privacy, his freedom, and, point in fact, his choice of life partner. He never chose to be an heir to a dynasty; rather, it was thrust upon him thanks to that outdated primogeniture nonsense. Who was to say he was any more deserving of the throne than his siblings, or even Darcy, for that matter? It all might have made sense a few centuries ago, but now?

He was beginning to wonder if being a relic of days gone by wasn't more of a strange curiosity that ought to be relegated to sideshow status or somehow set up as a tourist attraction to sustain the royal needs, of which there were plenty.

"Besides which, she's a complete drunk!" he whispered in his friend's ear.

"True, but you have to admit it was kind of hilarious when she took that spill down the grand staircase at your father's birthday party last month. Without that you'd have been left to listen to a string quartet as your only entertainment."

Adrian laughed. "Would have been preferable. And here I thought seeing her tumble head over heels down a flight of steps would have been enough for my mother to finally realize the woman's a total lush. Instead she bought into the whole excuse about Serena's blood sugar dropping so quickly, and Mother swoops in to care for her. *Bah!* Maybe if she'd eat a meal once in a while, she wouldn't be so embarrassingly smashed every time I see her."

"Obviously, she's head over heels for you," Darcy said, smiling. "What better way to prove it to you than quite literally showing you?"

Adrian moved into a smaller office within the confines of the larger one in which he was pacing, seeking a moment's solace from onlookers. He pulled Darcy close to him.

"Darc, I can trust you, no matter what, right?" he asked, his brow knit in concern.

"We're mates, Ade," Darcy said. "But you already know that!"

"And you don't want to see me stuck with Serena for the rest of my life, do you?"

"Are you kidding me? I'd practically marry her myself just to spare you," his friend said. "Although, honestly, I couldn't be that devoid of self-respect, so sorry, she's all yours." He chucked him in the arm, a sign of friendship he could only display amongst their closest of friends lest the "hired help" look like more. That whole propping up the royal stature thing really bugged Adrian, but Adrian was grateful that Darcy didn't mind at all.

"I need some space, Darcy," Adrian said. "I need time to think. And maybe to give my mother reason to care more about me as a person rather than a mere branch of the family tree that needs to be spliced together with what she deems to be an appropriate mate. I'm more than a glorified version of one of my mum's beloved horses, set out to stud to sire racehorse-quality offspring.

"I can't even stomach the *concept* of spending the rest of my life with Serena, let alone the reality of it. I'd give up my royal status and take a job waiting tables in a dingy pub before I submit to my mother's demands on this one."

"Good luck with that. You know your mother always gets what she wants. She's the queen, for God's sake."

"Maybe the queen needs to realize her once-little boy is a man now, capable of acting on his own behalf. And I'm going to start that right now."

"By?"

"By slipping away from here, unannounced. Getting out. Going somewhere. Doing something. For once not being led around with a bit in my mouth and a crop at my flanks. I need to get away, Darcy. And I need it now. I can't hide in Monaforte. But I can easily get lost in America. Think about it — it's a brilliant idea. Disappear for a while, see what it's like to actually live a bit."

"So you're running away from home then?"

"Don't make it sound so childish. It's nothing of the sort."

Darcy stood back and stared hard at his friend, his hands in his pockets, his shoulders back, his closely-cropped blond hair in direct contrast with the shiny black waves Adrian sported. He leaned forward and fixed his brown eyes to Adrian's blue ones.

"You're really serious about this, aren't you?"

"I think it's the first decision I've been serious about my whole life. I'm tired of living the life everyone expects of me. I need to see what it's like to just be *me* out there, Darcy. I really need you to help me escape. You can hold everyone at bay when they start asking questions. I know I'm asking a lot of you, but I swear to you I'll be safe and I will return, soon. But not before I discover who the hell I really am."

His friend stood, lost in thought for a few minutes, rubbing his chin with his thumb and forefinger, staring off into space. Finally he looked back at Adrian.

"You really think this is what you should do?"

Adrian nodded his head. "Look, not to slight you, but I don't think you can totally appreciate where I'm coming from. You're a marquess. If you decided to quit me, you could go back and lord over your father's estate and manage the family business. You aren't stuck as an appendage to the institution of the palace. You aren't carrying the weight of a country on your shoulders."

"You know one day I'll have no choice in that matter," Darcy said. "Once my father's gone." He looked down, and Adrian was sure he hated that idea, since he adored his father.

Adrian waved his hands, dismissing that concern. "Your father's healthy as a horse. It'll be years till it's your problem to deal with."

"We can only hope," his friend said. "Though yes, you're right, I don't have to partake in the dog and pony show of being the heir to the throne that you're stuck with. I get that. And you know I'm only here for you because it's you. We've been best friends since we met on the train on the way to boarding school when we were five. Hard to turn down a bloke I've known since his voice squeaked like a mouse."

"At least mine deepened into a man's voice," Adrian said, chiding him.

"Oh yeah? You think I still sound like a little girl?" Darcy said, making his voice go as high as possible.

The men laughed.

Darcy shook his head. "This goes against my better judgment. The queen would about kill me if she knew I was going to do this. Make that she would *actually* kill me. With her bare hands. But your wishes take precedence over hers for me," Darcy said. "If for no other reason than to spare you a lifetime of high-maintenance, low return-on-investment Serena, I'll do it."

Adrian looked puzzled, like he'd just been awarded a huge prize. "Seriously? You'll actually go along with this? You're not going to try to talk me out of it?"

"Christ, Ade. You and I practically finish each other's sentences. I've seen what your life is like. I know a lot of it is fun and games, beautiful women, fawning attention, but I also know how much pressure rests on you to always be perfect, to never fail your family, your adoring public, and your family."

He put air quotes around that "adoring" part.

"Yes, well, I do have a lot of adoring fans," Adrian said, mocking himself. "What with all those little old grannies who give me crocheted booties, begging me to produce a royal heir."

"Good lord, the last thing you need right now is a royal heir, particularly minus a royal bride. And I can promise you, Serena is *not* going to fill that void on my watch."

Adrian grabbed his friend by the shoulders. "You think we can make this work?"

Darcy buffed his nails on his chest as if showing off his prowess. "Are you kidding? With me as the brains behind this operation?"

"Perfect. Then how are we going to pull this off?"

"We? I thought this was your plan!"

"I don't have a plan, simply a need. I hadn't thought through how to implement the thing," he said. "How about we just work our way out of this holding room and I sneak out some back door, unnoticed. How hard could that be? There must be another way to slip out — maybe an employee entrance?"

Darcy chewed on this idea. He looked over to see a computer on a nearby desk. "Hmmm, let's see here," he said, walking over to the computer to see what he could find.

He typed in a bunch of keywords, trying a variety of searchable words until he finally found what he was looking for — a map of the building indicating various exits and detailing all rooms and spaces within.

"So much for national security. You can find pretty

much anything on the Internet these days," Darcy said, shaking his head. "Looks like you can work your way down this back staircase. Along this long corridor there appear to be a series of rooms. One would think there should be an unlocked room or two along there you could pop into to remain undetected, in case a security guard comes down that hallway. If nothing else there's always the loo." He pointed to the men's room sign.

He reached into the breast pocket of his cashmere overcoat.

"Here, take this," he said. It was his wallet, containing plenty of cash and credit cards.

"These are what you call dollars in America," he said with wink as he opened it wide to reveal a thick wad of bills.

"Ha-ha. Very funny. I'm not stupid, you know."

"So you like to tell me. But it's not like you've been out painting the town red on your own before."

"I'm not planning to paint anything red, or blue, or purple for that matter. That would draw a bit of attention, don't you think? Besides which, I'm not Zander."

Sometimes he wished he could be his brother Alexander, famously known as Zander, last year caught by paparazzi while cavorting naked in a Las Vegas swimming pool with a bevy of equally unclad, very young and very hot women. Seems you could get away with just about anything if you weren't the heir to the throne, and the worst that happened to you was a little tongue-lashing from Mother, once the tabloids had their fill of splashing the overexposing pictures across their front pages. And Zander could hardly have cared less.

Darcy shook his head.

"Just having at it with you, boss. Listen, I'm giving you my credit cards. The cash is from the palace anyhow — it's what I use as mad money when you need it. I don't want to give you the palace credit cards as they'd find you immediately if you used them."

He fumbled around in another pocket.

"Oh, and you'll want this." Darcy handed Adrian's passport to him. "I know you wouldn't be daft enough to leave the country, but it's always a good idea to have this on you just in case of an emergency. That way if you have to prove you are the future heir to the throne, maybe they'd actually believe you.

"Right now, I'm going to provide some pass interference for you. I'll tell the bodyguards that there's a woman involved and the two of you need some privacy, just to keep them at bay. I'll escort you to a lavatory and give you a chance to be out of the line of vision for enough time.

At that point, you need to follow this path, and get out fast. Once you're out, hail a taxi — you do know how to do that, right?"

"I think I can figure it out." Adrian rolled his eyes.

"Once you're in a taxi, you need to figure out a way out of town. You've got two phones on you: your official palace one, and your own private one that I lined up for you. You'd better hand over the palace version or else they'll find you in no time."

"You're so organized, you'll make a great mum someday." Adrian grinned.

"Please. I've got my hands full enough being your de facto governess. And that's why you're paying me the big bucks." He raised his eyebrows and pointed to his friend. "This is the most important thing: stay in touch with me. I am ultimately responsible for your well-being, so you owe it to me to keep the lines of communication open. You can call, you can text. Whatever you do, keep me apprised of where you are going and whom you are with. And most importantly, be wise about who you fraternize with."

"Fraternize? I'm going to find myself, not find a hook-up. Trust me, I sure as hell don't need to complicate things even more by adding a woman to the mix. Particularly an American one who lives thousands of miles away from me and hasn't a drop of royal blood—not to mention Monafortian blood—in her. Wouldn't my mother just love that?"

"Might be better if she at least has less liquor in her blood than Serena. Oh, I nearly forgot the most important thing. Just in case." He reached into yet another pocket. "Whatever you do, take these. The palace can't afford to have unwanted princelings popping up in the States nine months from now." He tucked a wad of condoms into Adrian's palm.

Adrian rolled his eyes. "Unnecessary optimist. Besides, I'm pretty sure I can keep my pants on for a few days."

"Well, I wouldn't be much of a friend if I didn't wish for you to get laid, now would I? Now, go, before I change my mind about this completely ill-conceived escape plan."

Chapter Three

NIGHT had long since fallen by the time Emma left the building. The breathtaking grandeur of the Library and the Capitol dome set against the darkening cobalt sky was something she never tired of. That, combined with twinkling Christmas lights from charming nearby row houses on Capitol Hill, made the view so beautiful that she decided to lean against a tree and just take in the scenery for a few minutes, enjoying the simple beauty of the moment.

She pondered what it was that had her so agitated about her work these days. After all, what better setting to work in? And what fascinating subjects, barring such exciting shoots as the morticians association annual meeting, which was coming up in a few weeks. Maybe it was just that feeling of wanting something more in life, maybe even someone to share it with. Though, ugh, so far sharing with someone hadn't exactly worked out, what with her last three boyfriends backfiring so spectacularly. Thank goodness Caro hadn't even brought up Gordon, bless his heart, who insisted he wasn't gay even after she found out he and his boyfriend had shared her bed when she was out of town last year.

Emma blew a tuft of hair out of her face, heaved a sigh, and pushed herself away from the tree.

She rifled in her purse for her keys, as she had a long walk to her car and liked to keep her keys at the ready just in case she needed to poke a mugger in the eyes unexpectedly. While she shook her purse trying to unearth the things, a hand closed over her mouth and an arm around her waist.

She gasped, ready to scream her lungs out, when a

familiar accented voice whispered in her ear. "Peas, peas, be quiet. It's me, Adrian. Whatever you do, don't scream. Please, don't scream."

Her heart raced like a hummingbird's. The only thing keeping her from fainting in fear was the recognition of that voice and her stupid comment being thrown back at her from earlier in the evening. But why? What? Huh?

"I'm so sorry. Believe me I'm not going to hurt you at all. I need you to turn around very quietly, please. I need your help desperately," the voice whispered, his breath so close to her ear she could feel her hair shifting with each word he spoke.

"Just turn around casually and pretend I'm a friend who surprised you, in case anyone's watching."

She knew no one was watching. She'd walked out a back exit to a virtually empty street just moments beforehand, save the occasional taxi cab speeding past. Her breath came fast, even as she told herself surely she was safe. It was only the prince. The prince? *The prince!* What would someone like him need from her? And why was he standing out on the street, alone, begging for her help?

She turned around and his hand slipped away from her mouth, though he then moved it down to clasp his other behind her back, securing her body close to his. If these were other circumstances and she wasn't being accosted by the guy, she'd almost think he was about to kiss her. Which wouldn't have been so objectionable, were she not still feeling a bit terrified.

"Would you mind telling me what the hell you are doing, your *highness*?" She put extra emphasis on the word, just to be sure he knew she was pissed. "You're lucky I didn't kick you in the family jewels. Considering your family, that might have been considerable." She laughed nervously at her own bad joke.

He rolled his eyes. He'd heard that family jewels joke about, oh, a bazillion times over the years. He did, after all, attend boarding school full of rambunctious and completely idiotic boys.

"Please forgive me, I'm so sorry. I said those words because I knew you'd immediately recognize me and not turn and spray mace in my eyes or something. Or kick me in a delicate location. Future Monaforte generations thank you for that, by the way. But truly, I'm so glad it's you I encountered out here."

Under what life circumstances would a handsome, wealthy, and famous young prince be glad to see her? She glanced around, expecting to have cameras filming this for some reality series, waiting for her to say something even more stupid than *peas to greet you, slur*, or whatever boneheaded thing lifted off of her tongue at that fatefully humiliating moment. *Definitely need to consider brushing up on conversational skills, lady.*

"And you're glad it's me because?"

"God, it's a long, long story. It has to do with Serena and my mother and I can't tell you everything now, but you need to know I have all of a few precious minutes in which to slip away before they send the hounds out after me, and I very much need your help."

"Hounds? And here I thought they were goons, those two apes lurking around you this evening."

He laughed quietly. "Yes, apes indeed. That's what my life comes down to, being followed around by a wall of human flesh to ensure I don't break the boundaries at all."

If she were a therapist, right about now she'd suggest he pull up a couch while she handed him a box of tissues. This story sounded like it could get good.

"So you want out, then?" she asked.

"That would be an understatement. I need to get away for a few days. I've got to figure things out, decide what I should do next, before the rest of my life is handed to me on a silver platter, like it or not."

"And I suppose this Serena chick has something to do with the silver platter?"

"Unfortunately, this Serena chick has a lot to do with it. Only make that a tarnished silver platter, in her case." He sighed. "As you can imagine, it's not so easy to be a public figure and attempt to find privacy. And right now, I very much need privacy. I know we don't know each other—"

"'*I know we don't know each other*'...If that's the most spot-on phrase of the night," Emma said. "Except for maybe that rockin' witty comment I blurted out earlier with the peas."

He laughed. "Oh, that was a good one. Believe it or not, people often say the stupidest things in front of me. Not that what you said was stupid. Okay, actually it was sort of stupid." He paused, and gave her a wink. "But people invariably become befuddled in front of royalty for some mysterious reason. They refuse to realize that we are human beings too, we eat the same way, we put our pants on the same way, we just happen to be—"

"Privileged?"

"Yes, privileged. I freely admit that. But enough of this now. I need to get somewhere, anywhere. I really don't care where. Just as long as I can get away and get some time to think. Any chance you'd be willing to help a stranger in need?" He batted his eyelashes at her, as if that would work on her hardened heart.

"Men," she said with a huff, rolling her eyes. "Honestly, the minute you want something you turn on the charm, and we're supposed to drop our pants for you?"

Adrian squinted his eyes in confusion. "I'm not asking you to—"

"I know, I know. Just an expression. My point is, dammit, I was so looking forward to going home and chilling out and not having to think. And now not only am I going to have to think, but I'm going to have to do it for two of us."

He looked at her, lower lip pouting out, eyes wide like a sad beagle.

"Oh, all right. Then let's get a move on. We've got to hoof it a few blocks if you want to get to my car before anyone recognizes where you are."

"I owe you, Miss—"

"Emma. Emma Davison. And no, you don't owe me anything. Consider it a humanitarian gesture for a new friend. Or welfare, for royalty." She reached out to shake his hand, in open defiance of that silly royal handshaking cooties rule. He extended his arm toward her, and they clasped hands for a moment, the warmth of flesh on flesh standing out against the cold night air. His fingers on hers were giving her flashbacks to their earlier meeting. And not in a good way. In a way that spelled trouble for a girl who was avoiding heartbreaker types.

"Emma, I'm most peas to greet you, yet again," he said, bowing with an exaggerated flourish, extending his arm out to the side. "And please, call me Adrian."

"Time to blow this popsicle stand," she said, handing him her camera bag. She reached down and pulled off her shoes, taking a heel in each hand. "If we're going to make any good time, these have to go. But you are going to so owe me a foot massage for this, buddy." And she wondered in what world would she have ever have expected to tell a royal houseguest that he needed to service *her*. How was that for role reversal?

Something in the Heir

She grabbed his hand and they began to run, and he ran as if his life depended on it, would even have taken the lead if only he knew where they were headed. But somehow he knew he was in capable hands with Emma in charge.

Get your copy of Something in the Heir, wherever you buy your books!

About Jenny

Jenny Gardiner is an award-winning #1 Kindle bestselling author who has published 37 novels, a memoir, and a collection of essays. Her work has been found in Ladies Home Journal, the Washington Post, Marie-Claire.com, Paste Magazine, and on National Public Radio. She is an occasional essayist on regional NPR affiliate WVTF-FM, and wrote a humorous column in Charlottesville's Daily Progress for over a decade as well as a food column for Cville Weekly Magazine. She has worked as a publicist for a United States senator, and as a freelance photographer, photographing such notable public figures as Prince Charles, Elizabeth Taylor, and the President of Uganda. She's been the volunteer coordinator for the Virginia Film Festival for ten years. She's really bad at math. Find her at www.jennygardiner.net